Marry Me, Cowboy

WILLOW WHITE

NEW CREATION PUBLISHING

Copyright ©2023 by Willow White

All rights reserved.

No portion of this book may be reproduced in any form without written permission from the publisher or author, except as permitted by U.S. copyright law.

This novel is a work of fiction. Names, characters, businesses, organizations, places, events, and incidents are either the products of the author's imagination or used in a fictitious manner.

Chapter 1

The explosion woke Wyatt from a sound sleep, but it was the cascade of splintering wood that made him sit up with a start and scan the living room, which was bathed in the blue light of the timed-out television. It took him a second to orient himself. He'd fallen asleep on his brother's couch again. He looked through the kitchen to the front door. What had he heard?

All he could hear now was the rain hitting the roof. He got up and went to the front window.

"What was that?" his older brother Hudson asked from behind him, flicking on a light.

"Turn that back off," Wyatt said shortly. "I'm trying to see outside."

Hudson obeyed, which surprised Wyatt. He must really want to know what was going on if he was willing to comply without giving Wyatt any lip.

"Oh my word," Wyatt said slowly as his brain figured out what his eyes were telling him.

"What is it?" Hudson came alongside him.

A glance told Wyatt that Hudson couldn't see anything; he didn't have his glasses on. "It appears that someone has driven their truck into the side of your barn." He could see the glow of their headlights through the cracks in the near side of the barn. "I'll go check it out." Wyatt went for his boots.

"Can you see the vehicle?" Hudson asked, now behind him, still staring out into the blurry night.

"Not really." Wyatt pulled on his second boot. "Just a tailgate. Looks old."

"He might have been drinking, might be ornery. Maybe we should call the sheriff."

Wyatt returned to his spot by the window and saw the driver for the first time. "Uh, she's not a he, and she doesn't look ornery." She looked gorgeous, though it was hard to tell for sure from this distance.

"Do we know her?"

"Not sure, not from here anyway. But she's wearing a wedding dress."

"What?" Chase said from behind them. "That's downright spooky." Chase stayed behind them in the shadows, showing no interest in viewing the chaos. "Is she a ghost?"

Hudson laughed. "I doubt it."

Wyatt knew that none of them believed in such things, but the scene in front of him *was* unsettling, and he was the only one who could see it. "She's just standing there in the rain," he narrated. "She's not moving. Maybe she's hurt." He didn't think so, since she was standing, not sitting or lying down.

"You're right," Hudson said. "She probably is hurt if she crashed into the barn. Old trucks don't have airbags. Let me go get my glasses."

"Only one of us has to get soaked. I'll bring her inside. And I'll holler if I need help." He stepped out into the wet and wind, pulling the door shut behind him.

She didn't turn toward him as he approached. He cleared his throat, so that he wouldn't startle her, but still, she didn't react. Maybe Chase was right. Maybe she was an apparition. He shook that disturbing thought out of his mind and scanned the area to make sure there wasn't anyone else there. "Ma'am?" he said when he got close enough to be heard.

Slowly, she turned. Black rivers of eye makeup ran down her cheeks. "Are you okay? Are you hurt?" He looked her over for wounds and didn't see anything. She looked healthy. Just very, very wet. Her elaborate gown clung to her body like saran wrap, revealing a rounded belly that could only mean one thing. She had a baby on board. Good grief, as if this situation couldn't get any stranger. They did need to get her to the hospital then, just to make sure the baby was okay. But first things first.

She was staring at her truck again now. "I think my whole life is over." She looked at him, sort of. It was more like she was looking through him. "Sorry to be so dramatic." She laughed, but he could hear bitterness in her voice. Whatever circumstances had brought her here, they weren't good.

"Let's get you inside," he said gently. He was tiring of the rain, so she must be.

"I can wait out here. Thank you, though. That's very kind."

"Wait out here?" he repeated slowly. It wasn't cold out, but it wasn't warm either, not with the rain and wind.

She didn't respond.

"What are you waiting for?" Had she already called for some help? In the middle of nowhere, in the middle of the night?

"The police." She said this matter-of-factly.

"You called the police?"

She turned her head to face him again. The rest of her body still hadn't moved. "No, I didn't. Didn't you?"

"No." He turned and motioned toward the house. "Come on, let's get you inside where it's dry and warm."

"Why didn't you call the cops? I drove into the side of your barn. There's obviously some expensive damage."

He looked at the barn. Yeah, there was some damage all right. She'd taken out most of one wall. "Eh," he said. "It's an old barn. We don't use it for much." He didn't know whether his brothers ever planned to use the barn for more. He didn't live here. Only Hudson and Chase did.

"Okay," she said suddenly.

"Okay?" He didn't know what she was agreeing to.

"I'm a little cold. I'll try to call ..." She didn't finish her sentence.

"Come on in. My brother's a doctor. He can check you over, make sure you and the—"

"You live with your brother?" She walked toward the house, her high heels sinking into the spring-softened ground.

"I don't. I fell asleep watching television. I've been here a lot lately, helping them out with some renovations. I'm a contractor." He couldn't tell if she was listening. "They just bought the place not long ago, so they're fixing it up a little." Not so much fixing it up as making it into what Chase needed it to be, but that was too hard to explain.

He hurried to open the door for her. Hudson met them at the threshold, fully dressed now and with his glasses on. Chase stayed back in the shadows. Wyatt was surprised he was visible at all. Chase liked to be invisible. Apparently his curiosity was overriding his anti-socialness for once.

Chapter 2

Olivia was in a daze. She couldn't believe she was still wearing the stupid dress. She hadn't loved it when she'd bought it. She never planned to wear it for quite so long. How humiliating. But she hadn't brought anything with her. She'd been so emotionally overwhelmed that she'd left everything at the wedding venue.

And now she was alone in the middle of nowhere South Dakota with three strange men, one of whom was lingering in the shadows like a complete weirdo.

"Any pain anywhere?" The smart-looking one was shining a light in her eyes.

"I'm fine," she managed. "Just a little chilled." She was more than chilled, but she knew there was nothing a doctor could do for what was ailing her. She shrank back from him to signal that she wanted the examination to end. He took the hint and busied himself taking his gloves off. A shiver tried to take over her body, and she tried to hide it. The original cowboy reappeared with neatly folded clothes in his hands. "My brother says you can use these. They're clean." He was still wearing his wet clothes. They were soaked. She felt guilty for making him stand out there for so long. Didn't his brother have some clothes for him as well?

She gingerly took the offered clothing. "Thank you."

He smiled at her, and she finally got a good look at him. Whoa, he was a looker! She cast her eyes down in a hurry, feeling silly for having such a thought under the circumstances.

The looker glanced at the smart looking one, who must be the doctor. "I can take her to the hospital--"

"No, no," she said quickly.

They both stared at her.

"I'm fine, and I don't have health insurance."

The looker glanced down at her stomach, and she crossed her arms in front of herself, self-conscious. "Uh, do you have a bathroom I could use?"

"Yeah, right this way. I'll show you."

She followed the looker into the living room. Then it was a straight shot to the bathroom. She really hadn't needed a tour guide, but it was sweet of him to be so thorough. She thanked him and stepped inside before turning to shut the door.

He stopped the door's swing with one hand. "I really think you should go to the hospital, just to be safe. You know ..." He said this conspiratorially as if they shared some secret.

If they did, she didn't know what the secret was. She looked him in the eye and tried to sound firm. "I'm fine." And then she shut the door.

Without meaning to she caught sight of herself in the mirror. She groaned. No wonder the looker thought she needed medical attention—she looked completely unhinged. Her hair, which had been meticulously coiffed only hours ago, was now plastered unevenly to her head. Her face was one giant black smear, making her look like a Navy SEAL ready to camouflage himself in a mud pit. And her dress—well, that was really the stuff of horror movies. It was plastered to her body, revealing, if not highlighting, every single unsightly curve. No wonder the looker had stared at her stomach.

She peeled the evil dress off her body as fast as she could and then kicked it into the corner, where it hit the wall with a loud *splat*. She had never hated anything as much as she now hated that dress.

She pulled on the sweatpants and sweatshirt. They were too big, but not by a wide margin. She grabbed a handful of Charmin Ultra Soft—these men had good taste, at least—and went to work on her face, but it was too big of a project for bathroom tissue and well water. She pulled bobby pins out of her hair, wincing more than once, until she got sick of that and then just resolved to leave the rest in there; then she pulled her wet locks into a twisted mass on the top of her head and angrily stabbed a few of the bobby pins back into place to hold it there.

She paused and looked herself in the eye. *What are you going to do?* she silently asked. What on God's green earth was she going to do? She didn't know, but the first step was probably getting out of this bathroom.

She reached for the doorknob, and her eyes caught on the stupid crumpled pile of lace and satin. She couldn't exactly leave that sitting there in the nice cowboys' house. Trying not to get her new sweatshirt wet, she picked up the sopping bejeweled mess and held it out in front of her like a dripping bomb as she opened the door and stepped out of the room.

"Uh ..." Wyatt reached to take the dress from her. "Not sure what to do with this ... but I can hang it up somewhere?"

"If you've got room in the rubbish bin, that'll work for me."

Wyatt hesitated. "Are you sure?"

"I'm sure," she said, her voice coming out almost like a growl.

He turned away from her, and the dress went out of sight, but she had a feeling he wasn't going to throw it away.

"Could I use your phone, please?" She didn't know who she was going to call, but it wasn't like she could stay here for the rest of her life.

Wyatt reappeared beside her with no dress and pulled a chair out for her. She sat, and he handed her his cell. "Is yours in your truck?"

"Uh no, it's ..." She didn't want to tell him that she'd left her phone at the wedding chapel.

Chapter 3

"Will you excuse me for a second?" the pretty woman in sweatpants said.

"Yeah, of course," Wyatt hurried to say. His curiosity was driving him nuts, but he tried to be patient. Who was she? Had she fled the scene before or after *I do*? Part of him hoped it was before, and her lack of a wedding ring supported that notion, but she wasn't wearing an engagement ring either, so he wasn't sure he should make assumptions based on her jewelry. And then he felt guilty for hoping anything. She was obviously pregnant. If she had run away from the baby's father, then that was not a good thing.

She carried his phone into the dark living room that Chase was no longer lurking in. Wyatt heard her mumbling and made a conscious effort not to eavesdrop.

"Any idea what her plans are?" Hudson asked. "I need to get some sleep."

"Didn't you join a group practice so that you wouldn't have to work on Sundays?"

"I don't have to work tomorrow," he growled. Apparently, in the middle of the night, Hudson was just as grumpy as Chase. "But that doesn't mean I want to be useless all day tomorrow because I spent all night standing in my kitchen. So I'm asking, what's the plan?"

How was he supposed to know the plan? "I don't even know her name yet. What do I look like, a mind reader? Go back to bed. I can figure out what she needs and how to help her." Hudson gave him a knowing look, one Wyatt didn't appreciate. "Dude, she's wearing a wedding dress."

Hudson polished off his herbal tea and set the empty cup on the counter before meeting Wyatt's eyes. "She's not wearing it anymore." He headed for his bedroom, patting Wyatt on the shoulder as he passed.

The woman was heading back into the kitchen, and Hudson tipped his imaginary hat to her. "Good night, ma'am. Wyatt here is going to take care of you." He flashed Wyatt an annoying smirk before going into his room. Wyatt was grateful that the woman couldn't have seen it. She looked suspicious enough as it was.

She handed him his phone back. "Thank you."

"You're welcome. Did you get a hold of someone?" He knew that she had, but he was curious who she'd called.

"I did, but it wasn't much use. They said they can't find a tow truck service in this area, and they said I have to file my insurance claim online."

It took him a second to figure out what she was talking about. "Oh, you were calling your insurance company?" He had assumed that she'd been talking to her mother or her maid of honor, or maybe even the man she'd recently married or almost married. He accidentally glanced at her left hand again, just to make sure he hadn't missed anything, and she caught him.

"I threw my engagement ring out the window on the way here. Not my smartest moment. I'm sure it wasn't worth much, but I could use even a few dollars right now." She sighed and looked around the room. "Anyway, yes, I was calling my insurance company because I am going to pay you for every penny of damage that I have done. I'm so sorry." She suddenly thrust out her hand. "Olivia, by the way. Olivia Long."

"Wow, that's a *long* name." He winced. "Sorry. That sounded funnier in my head." He shook her hand. "Wyatt Honeywood." He held his arms out to his side, trying to lighten the mood a little. "Welcome to Honeywood Ranch." His arms dropped with a soft slap. "It's not mine, but it belongs to my brothers, so I think I can officially welcome you."

"Those are both your brothers? The doctor and the ... other one?"

Wyatt chuckled softly. "Yeah. Hudson is the doc. And the other one is Chase. He isn't really a people person."

"I gathered."

They stared at each other for an awkward moment.

"So I don't know why the insurance company says they can't find a tow truck. I can find you one in the morning."

She smiled bashfully. "Thank you. I'd appreciate that."

He felt so bad for her. He didn't know what had happened, but he could feel her sadness from three feet away. "You don't have to wait here for the tow truck, though. I mean, you can, you can definitely stay here for as long as you need to, although it's not my house, but I'm pretty sure I can make that offer—" He forced himself to stop babbling.

She rubbed her eyes. "I'd ask you to take me to a hotel, but I don't have my wallet. It's uh ... with my phone."

He pulled out a chair and sat beside her. "And are your wallet and your phone at a church?"

"Yeah. Well no, we weren't going to get married at a church. We were at some supposedly swanky venue in the Black Hills. But it wasn't as swanky as the website suggested it would be." She took a deep breath.

"So you said you were *going to* get married? Does that mean you didn't?"

She laughed, and that same bitterness he'd felt outside wafted at him again. "Thank God, I did not." She looked up, and her wet eyes locked on his. "His girlfriend showed up. Turns out she didn't want to lose him to, you know, a *wife*."

Whoa. "I take it you didn't know about this girlfriend before then?"

Her *no* was short and crisp. "I most certainly did not."

What a creep. Wyatt ripped his eyes away from hers. She was gorgeous, but he couldn't go getting all attached. She was pregnant with another man's child. Wyatt wasn't sure what the moral path was here, but if he was going to figure that out, he was going to have to do it when he wasn't gazing into her eyes. "I'm so sorry," he said and cringed. What a lame thing to say. "So you just got in your truck and then what?" He chuckled. "Drove into our barn?"

She laughed too. "Someday I hope I can laugh about it without crying." She lowered her chin and rested it on her arms on the table. "I was so embarrassed and so angry that I just jumped into the truck without thinking, and I just started driving ..."

Interesting. She'd said embarrassed and angry. But she hadn't mentioned brokenhearted. Maybe she thought that part was obvious.

"So I drove around for a while, trying to figure out what to do, and I decided to head to my friend's house in Pierre, and I was really upset, been crying a lot, and I guess, somehow, I managed to fall asleep at the wheel. I hadn't slept much the night before either ..."

"Were you getting cold feet?"

She leaned closer to him as if she were about to confide something. "There were icicles in my shoes."

He failed to smother his laugh in time. "I'm so sorry. Sorry for laughing, and sorry that you ... that you've had to go through so much, especially when ..." It was probably rude to mention someone's pregnancy before she did, and he stopped himself just in time. She would tell him when she was ready.

"You don't have to be sorry," she said, sounding weary. "I'm the one who's sorry. I drove into the side of your barn."

He shrugged. "Ah, it happens all the time."

Her giggle was the most rewarding one he'd ever heard.

Chapter 4

Olivia wanted to keep talking to this kind, handsome man, but it was the middle of the night. "I should let you get back to sleep. I know you were asleep when I oh-so-politely knocked on your barn door."

Wyatt chuckled and then assured her he was okay. "And I meant it when I said that you didn't have to wait for the tow truck. I can just give you a ride home if you want?"

She shook her head quickly. "I don't have a home."

He raised an eyebrow. "You don't have a home?"

"I did have a home. I just don't anymore. At least I don't think so." She wanted to slap herself. Could she utter one cohesive sentence? She rubbed her eyes. She had never been this tired. "What I'm trying to say is that I used to live with … oh wow, this is so embarrassing. Turns out that being a runaway bride is an incredibly humbling experience." She forced a laugh, but it sounded hollow. Might as well come right out with it. "So I've been living with my fiancé's mother. That's right." She sighed. "I had a job and an apartment, but Brian made me quit the job ..." She wished she hadn't used the word *made*; it sounded so weak, but she didn't know how else to put it. "He talked me into quitting my job so that we could go on a long honeymoon, and I gave up my apartment because I had to save up money for the—" Her voice broke, and she stopped talking to avoid crying.

He nodded as if he understood, but she couldn't imagine how he could.

"Anyway, I'm not really sure what to do next. I mean, I'm sure I'll figure it out, but right now I'm a little out of sorts."

"Yeah, yeah," he said quickly, pushing back from the table so suddenly that she thought maybe she'd startled him. "I know you've got a lot of decisions to make, and I know they're not easy. Please don't feel any pressure from me. Hey, are you hungry? When's the last time you ate something? You must be hungry. You should eat."

She was hungry, but she was more tired. "I'm okay, thank you. I think I'd like to just take a nap." She looked over her shoulder into the dark living room. "Mind if I borrow your brother's couch?"

He chuckled. "No, I don't. But we even have a guest room. But really, can you please eat something? I could make you a sandwich? Or maybe some cereal?" He winced. "Sorry, I know those aren't very exciting offerings. Two bachelors live here. They don't cook much."

She smiled weakly. "I'm a cook. I mean, I was a cook, at a steakhouse, before I quit a job I loved for a honeymoon that was never going to happen."

He shifted his weight to his other foot. "So was that a yes to the cereal?"

She didn't want to eat. She wanted to sleep, but there was a weird desperation in his eyes; it was like he thought she was going to die if she didn't get some empty calories into her immediately.

He took her lack of an answer for a yes and went to a cupboard. "Hudson has really healthy stuff, all bran and flax and raisins and junk, but Chase is a little bit more reasonable in his cereal selections." He yanked a box out of the cupboard triumphantly. "Cocoa Puffs!" He looked at her, his eyes wide with excitement that she tried to mirror.

"Great. Thank you." She watched him pour too many rice orbs into a bowl and then smiled when he delivered the bowl to the table. He stared at her with such expectancy that she wondered if he was trying to poison her. "Aren't you having any?"

"Uh ... sure." He hurried to pour himself a bowl.

She didn't really think he was trying to poison her—he was too good looking to be a murderer—but she waited for him to take a bite just in case. He smiled at her foolishly as he crunched, a small drop of milk on his bottom lip. She dug in herself, and though she hadn't had Cocoa Puffs since she was about eight, the sweetness did cheer her tongue. She was too embarrassed to drink the milk from the bowl, but the thought crossed her mind. She got up and took her bowl to the sink, looking for a washcloth or sponge.

She felt his presence behind her suddenly, and he reached around her to take the bowl from her hand. "I'll take care of that later," he said softly. The moment was strangely intimate, and she was sad when he stepped back. "Come on, I'll show you to the guest room."

She followed him to the other side of the house and into a neat, small bedroom that felt oddly welcoming. He strode to the nightstand and clicked a lamp on. "It's not much, but it's yours for as long as you need it."

The bed looked so inviting. She thought she might sleep through till Monday morning if they let her. "It's so perfect. Thank you." Her voice cracked.

"You're welcome, and this is a private bathroom, too." He gestured to another door.

This was all too much. "I'm really sorry that I crashed into your barn. I'm too tired to figure it out now, but tomorrow, if I could use your phone again, I'll try to file the claim."

"Sounds like a plan. And really, it's okay. You've had a rough day. Try to get some sleep. It's not good for you to get overtired." He looked like he wanted to say more, but he didn't. Instead, he backed out of the room and shut the door, leaving her alone.

She had so much to think about. So much to process. So many decisions to make. But instead of all that, she climbed under the covers and promptly fell into a relieved sleep.

Chapter 5

"Why is she still here?" Chase glared at Wyatt, and Wyatt did his best to stand firm.

"She's not moving in, Chase. Calm down. It was the middle of the night. She doesn't have her purse. No ID, no money, no credit cards. It would have been downright unchristian not to give her shelter. What did you want me to do, throw her back out into the rain?"

Chase's scowl deepened. "I didn't say that. Don't put words in my mouth."

"Guys!" Hudson barked. "Are we going to leave her here or invite her to church?"

No one answered him at first.

"If she doesn't wake up on her own," Wyatt said, "I say we let her sleep as long as she can." He was thinking about the health of the baby, but he seemed to be the only one. He was starting to think that Hudson hadn't noticed that Olivia was pregnant, though that didn't seem likely. He'd had his glasses on and everything.

"We're just going to leave a perfect stranger here alone?" Chase said.

"Oh, will you stop!" Hudson said, no longer sounding so playful. "You only go to church half the time anyway."

"Well, I was planning on going today. But fine, I won't." He stormed outside, and Wyatt and Hudson exchanged a look. Chase could be taking this whole thing better, but he could be taking it a lot worse as well.

Wyatt busied himself making a second pot of coffee in case Olivia woke up and wanted some. He was watching it drip into the pot when Chase stormed back inside. "Have you *seen* the damage she did out there?"

Hudson hushed him. "Keep your voice down. We were talking about tearing that barn down anyway."

"We were only talking. It's a perfectly good barn. No one tears down perfectly good barns."

"It's an *ancient* barn," Wyatt said, "and she has insurance. You'll be paid for the damages."

"And are you going to be the one to repair it?"

Wyatt gave him a look that said of course he was.

"Fine." Chase turned to go back outside, which wasn't surprising. He had already said more than he usually said in a day, and it wasn't even nine o'clock yet.

"Hang on a sec, Chase." Hudson looked at Wyatt. "What is her plan? Are you going to help her get her wallet and phone back?"

He hadn't thought about those details yet. "I can help her do that. I also offered to drive her home. I'm waiting till nine to try to find a tow truck."

"On a Sunday?" Chase mumbled.

"Yeah. On a Sunday. Rodney will come out, I think. Then maybe she can drive off on her own. I don't know why you guys are acting like she's trying to move in. It was one night. Good grief, relax. Our mother would be having a fit if she could hear this conversation."

"We wouldn't be having it in front of her," Hudson admitted.

Wyatt was hit by the familiar stabbing pain of missing his parents. The room had fallen silent, and he knew his brothers were feeling their own personal versions of the same pain.

Chase took a deep breath. "So you'll take her to get her stuff today. Or home. Or somewhere."

"That's right." He had no idea what he was going to do. He was going to do whatever she needed him to do.

Chase narrowed his eyes. "Oh. Of course. Now I get it."

"Stop it—" Wyatt instantly knew where he was going and started to defend himself, but Hudson interrupted.

"We both know that Wyatt would show kindness to any woman, whether or not he found her attractive."

"Will you two keep it down, please?" Wyatt shot a nervous glance at the closed guest room door.

Hudson chuckled. "You might not want to get mixed up with a woman who just left a man at the altar."

Especially when she's carrying his child. "I can manage my own personal life, thank you."

Chase gave Hudson a wry look.

"Stop it! Both of you! Yes, she's beautiful, but ..." He didn't want to out her pregnancy. "But I promise you that it will never happen. Never *ever*."

Chapter 6

Olivia stood stock still with her hand on the doorknob. What had she just heard? First of all, Wyatt had called her beautiful. No one had called her beautiful since ... well, since her *father*. Brian had certainly never said she was beautiful. Not even close.

But then Wyatt had said *no way* with a downright offensive level of emphasis.

If he thought she was beautiful, why did he sound so horrified at the thought of dating her? Did he think she was crazy? She *had* driven into the side of his barn in the middle of the night wearing a wedding dress. She wasn't crazy, but she could see why he might have thought otherwise. Or maybe he thought she was pathetic. She imagined how she must have looked the night before, all that satin glued to her body. Yep, pathetic indeed.

She took a deep breath, steeled herself, and opened the door.

The guilt was written all over Wyatt's face. She smiled brightly to let him know that she had not overheard anything in the last thirty seconds. "Could I please borrow your phone? I'd like to try to file that claim."

Wyatt whipped his phone out of his pocket so fast that he bobbled it and then dropped it. She stifled a laugh as the cranky brother got up and went outside.

"Coffee?" the doctor offered.

Nothing had ever sounded so enticing ever. "Absolutely. Thank you." She tried to walk at a reasonable pace as she headed for the coffee pot. It would be embarrassing to sprint across the kitchen: she'd already embarrassed herself enough with these people; and she'd probably pull a muscle.

The doctor handed her a mug, and she thanked him. By the time she'd poured her coffee, Wyatt had recovered from his single-object juggling act and was handing her the phone. She thanked him as well and then carried the phone and coffee to the table.

She sat, feeling their eyes on her. She didn't know if she was going to be able to figure this app out, and she didn't really want them staring at her as she struggled.

But it wasn't as hard as she thought it would be; the hardest part was remembering her insurance password. She couldn't, so she had to reset it, which meant she had to visit her email account on his phone, and she couldn't remember that password either. But once she got all the passwords sorted, the app was easy to navigate, and she was able to file her claim.

She put the phone down and smiled at Wyatt, who was pretending not to stare at her. "Somebody will be here Wednesday to look at the barn. Sorry for the inconvenience."

Wyatt smiled brightly. "No inconvenience."

"And I will send you payment as soon as I can."

"Not worried about that either." He retrieved his phone. "It's after nine. I'll try to find you a tow truck now." He tapped at his screen several times and then held the phone to his ear.

Feeling weird for staring at him, she looked at Hudson. "I'm a pretty good cook. Can I make you breakfast? Try to repay some of your kindness?"

"No, thank you. We ate a while ago. But please help yourself to anything you can find."

"Okay, thank you." She didn't move. She wasn't hungry. She didn't usually eat breakfast.

Wyatt got off the phone. "He'll be here shortly."

She winced. How was she supposed to pay the tow truck driver without a wallet?

Wyatt read her mind. "He's a friend. He'll help us out, and we can pay him as soon as we find your wallet."

He made it sound like they were definitely going to find her wallet. She didn't know that to be the case. She didn't even remember where she'd last seen it. Someone at the venue had probably thrown it away by now. Or maybe worse. Maybe Brian was off honeymooning with her credit cards. Maybe she should call and cancel those.

"You said the wedding venue was in the Black Hills, right? Whereabouts? Maybe I could give you a lift there, see if someone has your wallet."

"Oh no, you don't have to do that." She didn't want him to do that. "Maybe the truck won't be so bad. Maybe I can just drive it."

Wyatt looked at her like she was crazy. "Uh … I'm pretty sure your truck is totaled."

Her heart sank. Her truck wasn't much, but it was paid for. She really, really hoped it wasn't totaled.

He saw her sadness. "Or maybe Rodney can fix it up, but if he can, it won't be a quick duct tape trick. It'll probably take some time."

"So then I will need a wallet."

He smiled. "Probably, yeah. And I would think that the sooner we try to get it back, the more likely we'll be to get it back."

So he had his doubts too. "Your reasoning is sound, and I thank you for that very generous offer …" What other choice did she have? She did have friends, of course, but it would take any one of them a while to get there and that was if Brian hadn't already turned them all against her. "I guess I'm ready to go when you are." She wasn't, but she was as close to ready as she was going to get.

"Are you going to skip church?" Hudson asked Wyatt.

"Yeah, just this once."

Hudson laughed, leading her to believe that Wyatt played hooky often.

She looked down at her sweats and her ridiculous high-heeled satin sandals. They'd once been the color of cream. Now they were mud-stained brown. They almost looked tie-dyed. She sighed. She couldn't believe she was about to go anywhere in this outfit, but she surely wasn't going to change back into that monstrous dress. In fact, her outfit was good motivation to get this chore over with. She had clothes at that venue too—and real shoes. "Okay, let's go then."

Chapter 7

Wyatt tried to think of something intelligent to say. The silence wasn't making him uncomfortable, but she seemed uneasy. Of course, why wouldn't she be? She was riding to the Black Hills with a complete stranger to visit the scene of her heartbreak. And she was pregnant. Surely that part was freaking her out more than she was letting on.

Thinking about that baby tied Wyatt's mind up in knots. He hated to think that she should marry a cheater, but shouldn't she be with the baby's father? It wasn't the baby's fault that his or her father was a jerk. Didn't the baby deserve a united household? Right and wrong had always seemed so black and white to Wyatt, but this whole situation seemed very gray.

Suddenly, he thought of a good question he could ask. "Were you and ..." He forgot the groom's name for a second, but then it came to him. "... Brian together for long?" If she said they'd only been together for six months, then he'd know that the jerk wasn't the baby's father, and he could stop wrestling with the ethics of the situation.

"Yes."

He almost laughed. That wasn't very helpful. Maybe she didn't feel like chatting. "Sorry, I was just trying to make conversation, but we certainly don't have to talk."

"No, I'm sorry." She exhaled forcefully. "I'm just so angry that it makes me a little crazy. And it's not even him ... well it is. Of course I'm furious with him, but I'm even madder at myself. I never should have been in that situation. I didn't know he would cheat, but I wasn't exactly head over heels in love with him either. So I shouldn't have been marrying him."

Wow, it was feast or famine with her, either one-syllable answers or pouring her heart out. "So, if I may ask"—now was his chance. She would share that she was pregnant, and he could stop watching his words and pretending he hadn't noticed. —"why were you marrying him?"

"Because I'm thirty-three years old, and I want to have a family before I'm dead."

Not exactly an admission, but he was getting closer.

"I thought, and I still think, that he would be a good father. He's basically a thirty-five-year-old kid. But if he's going to be a father, he's going to have to do it with someone else. I was willing to settle for him, but I'm not willing to share my husband."

Wyatt didn't know what to say. "You shouldn't have to settle."

"I know that's what all the romantics say, but in reality, women who wait for the perfect man often end up childless and alone."

He could not think of a single woman in that predicament, but maybe some of the women he'd assumed were happily married had in fact settled for less than they wanted.

She was staring at him. "You're single."

Was that a question? "Correct."

"And can I be super nosy and ask how old you are?"

"Sure. I am also thirty-three." And it had never occurred to him to panic that he was too old for a family. He'd been too busy working.

"So you don't want a family?"

"I definitely want a family. I've just been waiting for the perfect woman to come along." He flashed her a smile that he hoped was charming.

She laughed lightly. "Well, what's your idea of a perfect woman?"

You. He didn't quite have the courage to say it. Plus—the baby.

"Maybe I know someone." She was waiting for his answer.

"Well, she'd be beautiful, of course, and she'd know how to have fun. And she'd laugh at my jokes."

Olivia laughed.

"And while this isn't requirement exactly, I really would love it if she were a good cook because I really like to eat."

"I'm a good cook—" She broke off suddenly. "Sorry, I wasn't trying to volunteer for the gig. I'm not exactly a beauty queen, and I haven't had fun in years."

Really? Did she not know that she was gorgeous? If not, Brian was even more of a jerk than he thought. "Olivia, you *are* a beauty queen." His cheeks grew hot. Maybe he shouldn't have said that, but someone had to tell her.

She scoffed, "Maybe in a plus size pageant."

He tightened his grip on the wheel. He hated that she was being so hard on herself. She looked great. She looked healthy and huggable. "I've always liked a woman with curves. It usually means they appreciate good food, which means they can probably cook it."

She didn't say anything. She was suddenly staring intently at the fields rushing by her side window.

Whoops. Maybe he'd said too much.

"I do love to eat good food," she said softly.

"Maybe we could stop and get something on the way back. There are some good restaurants in Deadwood."

She smiled without looking at him. "Tempting, but only if we find my clothes. I don't think you want to be seen dining with Rocky Balboa."

He laughed. "I wouldn't mind, but yeah, I'm sure we'll find your clothes."

She didn't say anything for several minutes, and Wyatt felt hopeful. Maybe this really was going to be something. He could navigate stepfatherhood if that ended up being the right thing. "What do you do to have fun?"

"I really don't have fun."

He didn't believe that for a second. "No time for fun?"

She hesitated. "I've been working. I was saving for a house, and then I was saving for the wedding ..." Her voice trailed off, and he gave her a moment to finish her thought, but she didn't.

Why was she so reluctant to tell him she was pregnant? Was she embarrassed? Was she worried that he would judge her? Or maybe she liked him and was worried that the baby was a deal breaker. If that's what she was thinking, maybe he should set her straight.

"You'll probably have more fun once you have children. Kids are fun." She didn't say anything. *You idiot*, a familiar mind-voice jeered. Now you sound like a creepy kidnapper. "Anyway…" He cleared his throat and sat up straighter. "It's admirable that you worked so hard to save money. I've been accused of being a workaholic myself, but I'm not. Work is a good thing. What does Brian do? Was he saving for a house too?"

She groaned. "Brian thinks he's an entrepreneur. He's always starting new businesses and then walking away when they fail. I only invested in the first two. Then I learned my lesson."

Wyatt's jaw tightened. He really, really didn't like Brian.

"So no, he wasn't saving for anything."

"How was he going to pay for an elaborate honeymoon, then?"

"He won it through some contest that he paid a lot of money to enter."

Wyatt couldn't believe she'd almost married this guy, baby or no baby. The more he learned about the situation, the worse it got. "He should've opened a restaurant. If you're a good cook, that seems an obvious option."

"I suggested that at least a hundred times. He kept telling me that eighty percent of new restaurants fail. I didn't have the courage to tell him that one hundred percent of his new businesses fail, so eighty percent was a twenty percent improvement."

Wyatt laughed. "Is that something you'd like to do, open your own restaurant?"

"Maybe. I've sort of given up on that dream. I've given up on all my dreams, except motherhood. It's kind of weird to think I can start having dreams again."

"You should. Dreams are good." Wyatt could see a pretty sweet future stretched out in front of them. His contracting business plus her restaurant, cute little toddlers running around his living room.

He forced himself to consider the baby, the one that wasn't imaginary. "Where do you live?"

"Spearfish. Or I did. Born and raised."

"And Brian lives there too? He's trying to start new businesses in Spearfish?"

"Yes, he lives there, and no, his new businesses are online. He doesn't like to leave his house."

So the man had a house, at least.

"Or should I say, his father's house. He lives with his dad."

Wyatt tried not to laugh. "So you live with his mom, and Brian lives with his dad? You must have felt smothered by your soon-to-be in-laws."

"Yes and no. His mom really liked me. She knew I was a good catch for Brian. And she hated all his business foolishness. And it's important to me that you know that I didn't live with his mother for long. I just moved in there because I was really trying to save for the wedding, and I knew we'd be buying a house together after the honeymoon." She chuckled dryly. "I was actually looking forward to the honeymoon. I've never been anywhere."

"I really wasn't judging you for living with her. I get it."

She thanked him.

He hated how sad she sounded.

Chapter 8

"And there it is," Olivia said. "See what I mean? It's not even that great of a place. I mean the view is good, but that's it. Your ranch is nicer than this place. Maybe you should turn *that* into a wedding venue. According to my bill for this place, it can be a lucrative business."

Wyatt put the truck in park, and she reached for the door handle. Part of her was excited to get away from him for a minute and catch her breath.

"How can I help you right now?"

She stopped and looked at him, unsure of his meaning. He could help her by falling madly in love with her and letting her cook for him into their golden years. She almost giggled at the thought, but managed to hold it in.

"Do you want me to go in with you?"

"No, thank you." She had no idea what she was walking into. They might make things super simple, or they might be super rude to her. "And I'll hurry, I promise."

"Don't hurry on my account."

That was nice of him to say, but she did not want to keep him waiting. She shut the truck door, steeled herself, and headed toward the front of the building.

She didn't understand why this was making her so sick to her stomach. It was only a venue. She didn't know anyone here. And she'd only been here three times: once to see the place; once for her rehearsal the night before the wedding; and then yesterday.

She thought back to that rehearsal. She should have called it off then. Brian had been acting strange, constantly watching the door and mostly ignoring his bride to be. Now Olivia understood that his girlfriend had probably already threatened to show up.

She shuddered. She'd thought that he was her best option. Now she understood that remaining single was a better option than he had ever been. Maybe she wasn't supposed to be a mom. That would be okay, wouldn't it? Not her first choice, but she could still have a rich and rewarding life without a family of her own, right? Maybe she could move to some awesome, vibrant city and study under some phenomenal, famous chef. She could have afforded a month of that if she hadn't paid for this venue.

And all the food that probably never got served.

She arrived at the front doors, stopped, took a deep breath, reached out, and pulled.

Locked.

Oh no.

Had she really made the handsome cowboy come all this way? It *was* a Sunday. Why had she assumed they would be open? She glanced at the parking lot. Just as she'd thought—there were cars there. So then there had to be someone here, right?

She glanced back at the truck, but the reflection on his windshield prevented her from knowing if he was watching her.

Of course he was watching. She was like a one woman show. First act—crash into the barn. Second act—drive all the way to the Black Hills for nothing. She didn't want to know what fresh horrors the third act would offer.

She groaned. She wasn't giving up. She knocked on the door—loudly. Then she held her breath, listening.

There really wasn't anyone here.

No! She wasn't going to leave empty-handed. There had to be a back door. She stepped down off the porch, smiled brightly toward the truck in case he was watching, and then went around the far side of the building, looking for doors.

The first one was locked.

The second one was locked.

She climbed the steps to the beautiful back deck and peered in through the two locked glass doors.

No signs of life.

As she descended the stairs, she considered surrendering. Why not admit that she'd brought him on a wild goose chase? She'd already driven her truck into the side of his barn; it wasn't as if it could get any worse.

But then she saw it.

An open first-floor window.

She hurried to it, but when she reached it, it was a smidge higher off the ground than it had looked from her earlier position. She looked around for something to stand on. Was it too much to ask that someone had left a stepladder in the back yard?

She didn't see a step ladder, but she did see some molded metal chairs. She hurried to grab one. It was lighter than she'd expected it to be, and she wondered if it had ever been weight tested.

If not, this was the weight test. She easily carried it over to the window and then slid off her ridiculous wedding shoes so she could break in barefoot. She hoisted the window open the rest of the way. It made a loud creak as it slid up, so if there was someone there, she was probably going to get caught. She didn't care. Let them call the cops. She would definitely have grounds for an insanity defense.

She placed her hands on the sill, took a deep breath, and then jumped, pushing down on the windowsill with all her might, trying to throw her upper body forward. Her shoulder blade hit the top of the window and it let out a familiar creak. Oh no. She knew it couldn't open any further, so that creak meant only one thing—she hurriedly threw her hips back and forth trying to squirm her way over the sill before the window came down on her—and just when she had hope that she might make it, she felt the window's pressure on her back, just above her buttocks.

The old window wasn't all that heavy, but the weight was enough to stop her forward motion. She reached back with one arm to try to push it up, but her arm refused to bend at that angle. She could wiggle the window and make it creak, but she couldn't push it up.

Okay, fine. Time to abort the mission. She tried to wiggle backward, but she couldn't go that way either.

She stopped moving, her body a soft, bendy teeter totter. She kept her legs up in the air to keep some of the weight off her stomach, and she held her front half up with her abdominal muscles, which were fast losing their ambition. She surveyed her surroundings, looking for inspiration. Her head was in a sitting room of sorts, and she quickly took inventory: two hardback wooden chairs, a hutch full of knickknacks, and an unplugged vacuum cleaner. There was nothing useful. No large vat of Crisco, no handy time machine, and no fire alarm to pull to summon big strong men to rescue her while deepening her humiliation.

Her abdominals gave out then, and she let her upper half fall forward. It hurt the tender flesh on her stomach, but her burning muscles cried out in relief.

Her legs followed soon after, and her teeter totter transformed into a large, deflated, gray balloon. *What am I going to do?*

Think! You've been in worse predicaments than this.

She wasn't sure about that, but she appreciated her mind's attempt at a pep talk. One thing was for sure: she *had* to get out of this pickle before she completely lost circulation in her legs *and* before Wyatt finally got fed up with waiting and found her like this.

"Uh .... Olivia?"

Too late. She should have sawed her legs off.

"Hi." She tried to keep her voice light, but it was hard to talk. Her lungs weren't getting enough air, which explained the lack of oxygen in her legs. "You should know ... before driving into your barn, I led a pretty normal life."

She heard him chuckle. "I don't think I've ever had this effect on a woman before. You know, my mom was always a big fan of Calamity Jane. She would've liked you."

Olivia tried to groan and failed. "Your mother or Calamity Jane?"

"I meant my mother, but probably both."

"Calamity Olivia," she said, slurring her syllables together. "Doesn't have quite the same ring."

"No, no, it doesn't. So, I'm happy to pull you or push you. Which way would you like to go?"

The idea of him pushing *or* pulling on her bottom horrified her. "Uh ... I don't think I need either. If you could just push the window up, I think I can manage to ..." Goodness, talking was a lot of work. "I just sort of got pinned."

"Yeah, I hate it when that happens. Okay, let me see what I can do." She felt his body—close—but he didn't touch her. And then she felt the window lift off her back, and as the pins and needles exploded into her legs, she immediately started wiggling like a giant worm fleeing a scorpion.

She was in such a hurry to get away from the cowboy that she overshot her goal, lost track of her center of gravity, and plummeted head first into the sitting room. Her left shoulder hit the floor, and the rest of her soon followed, making a loud crash that shook the room. She cried out in grief more than pain and then slowly tried to untangle herself.

"Are you okay?"

She looked up to see his head sticking in through the window. He'd taken his hat off. He was smiling like he was having a great time. He'd said he wanted a woman who knew how to have fun. Oh boy was she fitting the bill.

She wished the floor would open up and swallow her.

She laid her head back on the carpet and closed her eyes to rest for a bit but then remembered the mission she had to complete. She got up and looked around, trying to get her bearings. Where was she in relation to the dressing room? "Okay, I'll be right back. For real this time." She hurried away from him, relatively sure of where she was going. She tripped over the vacuum cleaner cord, but, thank God, didn't fall, and then she was out of the room and in a narrow hallway that she recognized. Now she just needed to get her stuff and then get back through that tiny window without getting caught. Good thing she'd gone on that brief wedding dress diet. She'd needed it more than she'd thought.

Chapter 9

Wyatt had worked so hard to stifle his laughter, but now that he could let it out, he'd lost the urge. He watched Olivia disappear in the shadows of the venue and tried to rein in his emotions. He really liked her. Not only was she beautiful, but she was so much fun. Sure, she probably hadn't meant to get stuck in a window like the world's clumsiest cat burglar, but still—the entertainment value was there whether intentional or not.

He scanned his surroundings looking for witnesses, but all was quiet and still. He didn't think they'd get thrown in the clink for this escapade, but he didn't really want to explain himself to the owners of this place or to the sheriff.

Olivia was right, though. This really wasn't that fancy of an establishment. He didn't know what it had been in its first life, but someone had built a large, oddly shaped house way out here in the boonies, and then someone else had decided it should be a wedding venue. He noticed a change in the foundation and realized that maybe it hadn't started out as an oddly shaped building. At some point someone had decided it wasn't big enough and had added an addition.

He loved looking at buildings of all ages and wondering about the minds and hands that had created them. Each building was as unique as a person with its own stories. He was still pondering the addition when an arm was thrust out the window.

He took the outstretched wallet and phone, and then she handed him a small duffel bag. He looked into her wide eyes. "Okay, let's blow this popsicle stand, shall we?"

She stared at him. "Blow the popsicle stand?"

He chuckled. "I'll explain in the truck. Let's get out of here."

"Okay." She hesitated. "I'd like to save some face, though I don't know if that's possible at this point. I'm not sure I'm coordinated enough to go out feet first, and I don't want to try headfirst and then need you to pull me out by my armpits like a toddler stuck in a highchair."

It was really hard not to laugh at the image those words conjured, but he managed. "Or you could just go out the door. I doubt they're all locked from the inside."

Her expression made it clear that she hadn't thought of that. "I don't want to set off any alarms."

He smiled and then looked up at the wall of peeling paint in front of him. "In this place? Nah ..."

She considered her options.

"Go ahead. Try the front door. If an alarm goes off, we'll be long gone before anyone answers it." He held up her wallet. "I'll take these and meet you at the truck." He waited for her okay and then headed up the slight slope to the parking lot. He probably didn't need to be carrying her things if she was going to come out through a door, but it would have been even weirder to hand them back in through the window to her.

She was outside before he'd reached the front of the building. "You were right. Sorry."

"Nothing to be sorry about," he said quickly. "I can see why you thought you'd have to break out, seeings how you had to break in."

She chuckled. "I can't believe I did that. Hey, my phone is dead. Mind if I plug it in?"

"Help yourself." He started the engine.

"Why'd you call it a popsicle stand? Is that some kind of insult?"

"Something my mother used to say." He pulled out of the lot before continuing. "I'm not sure where it's from. I think it came from some crazy guy from Jamaica who wanted to use popsicles to kill people."

"What?"

"Yeah, now that I think about it, it's not as funny as it sounds."

"Well ..." She dramatically waggled her phone in the air. "Now that I have a phone again, I can look these things up. Well, as soon as it turns on, anyway." She let out a little shriek.

"What? What is it?"

"Uh ... I don't suppose you grabbed my shoes?"

"What shoes?" He looked at her feet, and she was wearing tennis shoes he hadn't seen before. Then he remembered her soiled wedding shoes.

She groaned. "I left my super awesome satin sandals outside the window."

He couldn't hold in the laugh this time. "Do you want me to go back?"

"No. If they dust them for prints, and I get thrown in the slammer, at least I'll have a place to live."

"I don't think that's going to happen. They were kind of destroyed anyway, weren't they?"

"They sure were. It's not like I was going to save them for my daughter or anything."

He held his breath. This was it. She was going to tell him.

Her phone chimed, and she gasped. "Oh my word, I have eighty million messages."

Okay, so she wasn't going to tell him. And Brian had sent her eighty million apologies. Maybe Wyatt had to *stop* having a crush on her. This obviously wasn't meant to be. Maybe this whole thing had scared Brian into acting like a real man and taking care of his family.

"I'll deal with those in a sec. First I have to find out about the popsicles. I used to make some crazy good popsicles once out of lime juice and maple syrup."

His mouth watered. "Maple syrup is pricey. Not a lot of maple trees around here."

"Yeah, I've got cousins east river who make some, but I used the gross store brand, but anyway ..." She giggled as she read. "Says here that it originated in an old gangster movie from the thirties. Some gangster was trying to insult a bar, saying that their booze was actually pop, and so they were going to leave."

"What?" Wyatt felt foolish. "For real?"

"I don't know. Sounds as plausible as the Jamaican terrorist." She looked at him quickly. "We should come up with an even more ridiculous origin story and then post it all over the Internet."

He chuckled. She was avoiding reading her messages. "I'm not sure I'm that creative."

She narrowed her eyes, thinking. "We could say that some naughty kids from east river were mad that their popsicle stand didn't have any lime and maple popsicles, so they bombed the place."

"I'm not sure that would work. The phrase means to leave a place, not to blow it to smithereens. Besides, have you ever actually *seen* a popsicle stand in South Dakota?" Wyatt's phone rang. His truck told him that it was Rodney calling. "Hey, it's the mechanic. I'm going to answer." He pressed a button on his steering wheel and said hello.

Olivia stared at the dashboard expectantly.

"Hey, it's Rodney. I've looked that truck over."

"Great. Thanks for doing that on a Sunday."

"Don't tell my mother. I knew your visitor was in a hurry—"

"You're on speaker phone with her right now. What'd you find out?"

Rodney's tone turned a touch more professional. "She might want to have her insurance guy look at it. It's repairable, but I'm not sure it's worth the investment. Might be better just to take the check and start over. It's an old truck."

Wyatt glanced at Olivia, trying to read her reaction and giving her time to say something. When she didn't, he said, "Thanks, Rodney. We'll get back to you soon."

"Okay, yeah. No problem. Just let me know what you want to do."

"Will do." He hung up and looked at her again. "Sorry. I know that wasn't the news you wanted."

"It's an old truck, and that would be a small check. I don't think I can get a car loan without a job, and I don't want to have a car loan." She leaned her head back on the headrest and closed her eyes.

Wyatt hated seeing her so defeated but couldn't think of anything to say to cheer her up.

"Why oh why did I have to fall asleep at the wheel and smash into your barn?"

Wyatt didn't know, but he wasn't exactly sorry that she had.

Chapter 10

Olivia didn't know what to do. She wasn't good at making small decisions let alone these big tricky ones. She decided it would be easier to face her many messages than to deal with the truck news. She opened her message app and started reading.

She groaned.

"Not good?" Wyatt asked.

"I should have asked your friend for an estimate." Somehow, reading the messages gave her clarity on her other crisis.

"Go ahead." Wyatt pulled his phone out of its holder. "Send him a text and ask him."

When she took the phone from his hand, her fingers accidentally brushed his, and sparks zinged up her arm. She hurriedly turned her eyes to the phone. Its screen had about a thousand tiny cracks in it.

"Sorry. It's been dropped off a lot of ladders. I stopped paying for new screens about the fifth time I broke a new one."

She laughed. "You like doing what you do?"

"I really do. I like to build things, but mostly I just like to see things built. Gives me a sense of accomplishment."

"That's very cool." She was a bit envious. She couldn't remember the last time she'd felt accomplished. She shot the mechanic a quick text and then went back to her own phone. "Wow, people are really mad at me."

"People?"

"Yeah. Our friends. Guess they were never really my friends at all. And he obviously didn't tell them why I ran off, only that I did." She sighed. Her head was starting to hurt.

"Anything from him?" Wyatt asked tentatively.

She was surprised that he cared. She sighed. Did she really want to share this with him? So far, he'd been a nonjudgmental sweetheart, but she wasn't sure anyone would be able to keep up with this saga without eventually judging her. "Yeah. He says that he's sorry that I had to find out that way."

"Wow."

She waited for more, but Wyatt had apparently been struck speechless. "Yeah. Wow is right."

"So he's sorry that he cheated on you. Not sorry that he ruined your wedding. Not even sorry that you found out. Just sorry that you found out *that way*." He actually sounded angry, which she found quite endearing.

"Yeah. That's pretty much it."

Wyatt glanced at her. "And has he always been like this, or is he having some sort of premature mid-life crisis?"

"No ..." She sighed. "He's pretty much always been like this."

"Okay, not to be harsh"—he sounded like he was going to be harsh, and she braced herself for the judgment— "but what were you *thinking*? Olivia, you are smart and beautiful and funny ... don't want to freak you out, but you're quite a catch, and this guy sounds like such a creep! He must be the best-looking guy on the planet!"

She guffawed so suddenly that she hurt her throat. "Uh, no."

"No?" He was staring at her, waiting for her to make it make sense.

"No. He looks like a stubby toad." The laugh bubbled up out of her so suddenly that it almost hurt. After a stunned pause, Wyatt joined her in her laughter, and as weird as the moment was, she felt some of her stress sliding away from her.

"Well, I'll admit that I don't know you very well yet." Wyatt wiped at his eyes. "But you seem far too cool of a woman to be mixed up with a stubby toad."

She didn't know what to say. There was no way this guy was interested in her, right? But either way, she didn't know men who said things like this, or even *thought* things this nice.

"Sorry," Wyatt said, sounding regretful. "I didn't mean to freak you out. I know you've been through a lot. I'm not trying to be your rebound or anything. I just wish you could see your own value."

Her throat grew thick. "I'm not freaked out," she said with difficulty. "And thank you for saying such nice things." Suddenly she was embarrassed. This guy already thought she was a clumsy fool. She didn't want him also thinking that she'd spent her whole life wallowing in low self-esteem. "It wasn't always like this. In fact, it's not like it right now. It's not as bad as you think it is. I have healthy self-esteem. I'm a confident woman." She could feel his disbelief from across the cab. "I'm serious. It's true."

"I believe you. Obviously, I'm not getting to know you on the best weekend of your life."

She laughed. "Thank you for making me smile. And no, you met me on a very, very bad day. I used to sort of have the world by the tail, but man, dating is hard." She waited for him to agree with her, but he didn't. She stared at him. Expectantly.

"I wouldn't know. I don't really try."

That explained it. She'd been wondering why he was single. "Well, take my word for it. It's kind of awful. And I've just worked really hard my entire adult life and not gotten anywhere. I feel like I've been treading water and all I've got to show for it are tired legs. And then one day I woke up and I was thirty and I sort of panicked. I thought that I'd be married with kids by then."

"Thirty isn't old," he said pleadingly. Maybe he was trying to convince himself as well.

"I know. And I didn't feel old. I just felt really ready to have a family."

"I can understand that," he said softly.

Chapter 11

Wyatt opened the gas station door for her and let her go inside first. She had refused to go into any restaurant wearing Chase's sweatpants. And though Wyatt wouldn't have minded being seen with her in sweatpants, he also couldn't blame her. He paid for some gas and went outside to pump while she changed in the restroom.

When she came outside, she looked like a new woman. She put her hair up into a bouncy bun on top of her head, and it turned out that pastel pink was really her color. She wore tight jeans that accentuated her curves in all the right ways, and he had to pull his eyes away. He forced himself to look at the rapidly climbing dollar amount on the gas pump.

When he got into the truck, he asked, "Feel better?" even though he knew the answer.

"I sure do. It's amazing what a good pair of jeans can do for a girl."

He laughed. "It's the same for a guy. Well, maybe not. I can't say I really know what it's like for a girl." *Stop babbling, you idiot.* "Anyway, how about Maverick's? Oh wait, you said you were a cook at a steakhouse. Are you sick of that kind of food?"

"No, that sounds good. I've never been there."

"We could go to Chubby Chipmunk after."

Her laugh was staccato. "Are you serious?"

He didn't understand. Was he serious about fancy chocolate? Yes, of course. He was trying to be nice to her.

"Is that really a thing? It sounds like a fat joke."

"Yes, it is really a thing. A very, very good thing." He tried to study her without getting caught. Did she really think she had a weight problem? Because she didn't. She was perfect. "It's a candy store. The best chocolates in the state, I'm pretty sure. They've got this Hot Mama truffle that makes me about cry with joy. It's got a bunch of hot peppers inside the world's best chocolate."

"First it's the state's best. Then the world's. Must be pretty good chocolate."

"It is. And I'll prove it to you." Suddenly he was ravenous.

It was easy to find parking in downtown Deadwood so early in the spring. It was a good thing she hadn't crashed into his barn during Wild Bill Days or the Motorcycle Rally.

They were seated right away at a cozy table in the corner, and now that he was seated across the table from her, he felt like he was on a date, and this made him nervous. He hadn't been on a date in a very long time. "Would you like to get an appetizer?" He expected her to say no. While he hadn't been on very many dates in the past few years, he had noticed a pattern with the ones he'd been on: the women didn't eat anything. Each of them had ordered a meatless salad and then picked at it nervously. There was nothing wrong with this, of course, but he'd wondered what he was doing wrong, what he'd done to make these woman lose their appetite, or even worse, what he'd done that made them afraid to eat in front of him.

Olivia promptly broke the pattern. "I'm starving. Let's get the chislic. But don't worry ..." She held her wallet up in the air and wiggled it. "It's my treat."

He would rather walk over hot coals than let her pay for her own chislic, but he didn't say so yet. "I'm partial to their gunslinger rolls, so let's get both."

"Deal!" she said with great cheer. Yep, she was a pattern breaker. It made sense. She was the first woman to crash into his brothers' barn as well.

She put her menu down and smiled at him.

"What are you going to have?"

"A salad."

Oops. Maybe not such a pattern breaker after all.

"Just kidding!" she cried gleefully. "I'm having the tortellini Alfredo with Cajun steak."

"Oh wow, sounds good."

"Yes, I expect it to be an adventure for the palate."

He narrowed his eyes. "Are you doing research right now?"

"Who me?" she said with theatrical innocence.

"Yeah, you, the cook. Are you going to pilfer their recipes for your future restaurant?"

She sighed wistfully. "I try not to dream about impossible things, so no, I don't plan to pilfer anything, but I am always doing research. I can't help it."

"Owning your own restaurant is not an impossible dream."

"Maybe not. Honestly? I'm not sure I'd even want to. It sounds stressful. I think I'd rather be a famous chef at someone else's restaurant, someone who pays me a lot." She laughed. "Then I could get days off. Either way, I am always looking for new food ideas. They are exciting, whether I ever use them or not."

"And Alfredo Cajun chicken"—he couldn't remember the dish's name—"is a new idea?"

"Well, nothing's new under the sun, but no, I've never had Cajun steak in Alfredo sauce. I expect it to be spectacular." It was so sweet of her to gently correct him on the dish she'd ordered.

Wyatt had to pull his eyes away from the lovable light in Olivia's eyes. He'd always loved food, but Olivia's love for food made him love it even more. *She is pregnant with someone else's child. She should probably be with him.*

She opened her wallet, rifled through it, and looked stressed out.

"Is something missing?"

"No, no. I just couldn't remember how much cash I had."

His resolve to pay for their meal strengthened. "Just in case this isn't clear, you're welcome to stay at the ranch until Rodney finishes your truck, even if you did get your wallet back."

"That's very kind of you, but isn't it your brothers' ranch?"

"What? You don't think I can speak for my brothers?"

She giggled and narrowed her eyes at him.

"You're right, I can't. But Hudson has made it clear that you're welcome there."

"But doesn't the ranch belong to Hudson *and* Chase?"

"It does, but don't worry about Chase. He's more bark than bite."

"I'm not really into being barked at either."

Wyatt chuckled. "He's been through a lot. When he got out of the service, Hudson helped him buy the ranch. We all wanted him to have a good place to reacclimate."

"With horses," she added.

"Yes, exactly. With horses. Chase loves animals, especially horses."

"How many does he have?"

"Not many yet, but he's pretty selective because he's looking for breeding stock."

"Is that the plan?"

"It was. I'm not sure if it still is. It's been slow going."

"Because he's so picky?"

"Yes, and because it turns out that raising horses is a bit pricey."

"Oh." She looked and sounded sad.

"No, it's all good. He's happy. Well, as happy as Chase can be, anyway. It's all good. But yeah, Hudson's medical career is sort of paying for the ranch."

"Have you guys always lived in West Hope."

"We have, but not on a ranch. We lived in town, but Chase used to help out at a friend's ranch, and he was always involved in 4H growing up. How about you? Did you grow up in Spearfish?"

She groaned, and the light left her eyes.

"What? Not a Spearfish fan?"

"I just ... yes, I've always lived in Spearfish, and all my stuff is still there. I just realized that I have no idea what to do about that."

He shrugged. "I guess we should go get it."

"Yeah, like you haven't driven enough miles for me yet."

"This is South Dakota. We are all used to driving miles."

She looked bashful all of a sudden. "You don't have to do that."

"You know what?" He slapped the table. "I just thought of an errand I have to run, and it so happens to be in Spearfish. What a happy coincidence!"

She narrowed her eyes. "Well, isn't that convenient."

He smiled, quite proud of himself.

"Thank you. You are incredibly kind."

Chapter 12

Olivia let the salted dark chocolate truffle dissolve in her mouth, trying to make it last as long as possible. Wyatt had purchased half the chocolate store, but still, it was so good, she wanted to make it last forever.

She couldn't believe that this man was driving her to Spearfish. For someone who would "never, ever" date her, he was certainly acting like he liked her. She kept analyzing this so that she wouldn't think about what was going to happen when she arrived in Spearfish.

She had always had a great relationship with Brian's mother, so much so that she would often complain about her son, taking Olivia's side when he was being ridiculous—but she didn't think the woman was going to side with her this time. She very much doubted that Brian had admitted his affair to his mother, or to anyone.

Maybe she should have made more of a scene at the wedding, screamed her head off, shouting that woman's name, stomped around flipping tables over. It was a fun fantasy, but she hadn't done any of that. She'd just left.

"Are you okay?"

"Oh yeah. Sorry. Just don't really like confrontation, and I think I'm about to have one."

"Do you think Brian will be there?"

"I'm almost sure that he won't, but I don't really want to have to face his mother either." She didn't want to sound like a whiner, so she hurried to add, "It'll be okay, though. I'll just quickly gather my things and then get out of there one last time."

"I can go in with you if that would help." His tone betrayed his hesitation. He wasn't sure if he wanted to commit to that.

"I don't think that will be necessary, but thank you. She's a nice woman. She won't be awful or anything. I just ..." Her voice cracked. "I grew to care about her, and I don't really want to face her. I don't like disappointing people."

"Olivia, none of this is your fault. If she's got any sense at all, she's going to know that he's the one who blew this."

"Yeah, she'll know, but I think that would be a hard thing for a mother to face."

"Do you have any family of your own left in Spearfish?"

"I haven't seen my father in more than twenty years. I lost my mom when Brian and I first started dating. I've got some cousins and an aunt that I never really talk to, but that's it.

"Small family."

"Yeah. My father's family was big, but I haven't seen any of them in a long, long time. I don't think I'd recognize them if I saw them in the grocery store."

It occurred to her why he might be asking. "I do have a few friends in town, people I grew up with, as opposed to those people I was friends with only because of Brian. Maybe I should ask one of them if I could stay with them." She didn't want to do this, but it would be nice of her to get out of the Honeywood brothers' hair. They had done enough for her already.

"Only if you want to. I promise that Hudson doesn't mind. And your truck is still in West Hope, don't forget."

"I know, but I'm sure one of them could give me a ride to the garage when it's ready." She was sure of no such thing, but it sounded good. "I haven't talked to any of them in years. When I first got together with Brian, he became my whole world, and I just stopped having friends. Back then, I thought that was normal, but looking back on it, now I wonder if it was intentional on his part. It seems like he never wanted me to have any friends of my own."

"I'm so sorry."

"It's okay." It wasn't, but she was feeling better with every minute away from him.

They rode in silence for a few minutes, but then they were almost there, and she started giving him directions, her stomach swarming with nerves.

"That must be it," he said.

It took her a second to realize what she was looking at. Her first inclination was that Brian's mother had decided to have the world's messiest yard sale. But then she realized that it wasn't a yard sale. It was her stuff.

She'd been moved out.

Her clothes were strewn all over the lawn. Boxes lay on their side, contents spilling out. Her cookbooks lay open, their recipes pointed at the sky. Photo albums lay flat in the sun.

"What's Brian's mom's name?" Wyatt muttered.

"Connie."

"Hmm. That doesn't seem to fit." He sighed. "I don't care what you say. *Connie* is not a nice woman, and I'm going in with you."

"I'm not sure we have to go in at all." Tears spilled out her eyes. She felt so betrayed, so disrespected. She really hoped that the woman hadn't thrown the stuff out the night of the wedding. If it had rained in West Hope, it had probably rained here.

She got out of the truck and tentatively picked up the first cookbook. Sure enough, it was soaked. A sob burst out of her before she could check it.

She clumsily righted a large box and started shoving her sodden belongings into it. There was standing water in her jewelry box, and some of it was missing. Had Connie stolen her jewelry? She didn't see why she would. It wasn't expensive stuff.

Wyatt was watching her. "Is stuff missing?"

She nodded. "But I can't believe she'd take it. It was just cheap stuff."

"She probably didn't, but if it's been out here for a while, probably someone's rifled through it."

The thought made her sick.

"Sorry, I shouldn't have said that." He slowly reached up and laid a warm hand on hers, pausing there before gently taking the jewelry box from her trembling hands. He stepped closer. "Why don't you go sit in the truck? I can get this." He reached out and tipped her chin up with two fingers, and for one insane moment, she thought he was going to kiss her. "Keep your chin up. Don't let them see you sweat."

She could smell him. He smelled like wood shavings and clean laundry. She had never wanted to kiss a man so bad in her life—she leaned into him and pressed her lips to his with a desperation that stunned her. His lips were warm and—

He yanked away, his eyes wide, studying hers.

"Sorry," she muttered.

"Go ahead and get in the truck," he said, his voice void of emotion. "I'm right behind you."

Now on top of her heartache and her horror, she was embarrassed too. She'd *kissed* him? What on earth had she been thinking? He didn't want her to *kiss* him! This was the "never ever" guy! Her legs felt like giant bags of sand that she was dragging toward the truck, but she made it. She opened the door and hoisted herself into the seat, and that's when she saw him: Brian. Striding across the lawn toward Wyatt. Her heart twitched with an echo of longing. She really had loved him in a way, in a way she'd talked herself into. She hadn't believed he would cheat on her. She'd thought he'd be a good husband, a good dad, but now he really did resemble a red-faced stubby toad. She left the door open so she could hear what he had to say.

He swore and then asked Wyatt who he was.

Wyatt, to his credit, didn't even look up. He just swiftly continued to put her things in boxes.

Brian was still spewing nonsense when Wyatt straightened with a box under each arm. He turned toward the truck, and Brian's eyes followed his path. That's when Brian's eyes met hers for a brief lock before she looked away. Then she wished she hadn't. She wanted to look strong, so she forced herself to look at him, but his eyes were back on Wyatt.

Wyatt didn't look at her. He put the boxes in the back of the truck and then headed back for her clothes. He didn't bother boxing these up. He just draped them over his arm. She about wanted to die when he hung one of her best bras off his fingertips. The whole time, Brian continued to holler, pointing at the road and telling Wyatt to get off his property. This was so insane. It wasn't his property. Maybe she should do something. But what?

She was grateful to realize that Wyatt was going to be able to load all of her stuff up in only three trips. That's all she had to show for this life—three trips to a pickup. Everything she owned fit into an eight-foot bed, and easily at that.

Just when she thought that Wyatt was going to get out of this whole ordeal without speaking to Brian, he squared his body to him, tipped his hat back, and put his hands on his hips. Brian shrank back and shut up.

"You sir," Wyatt said frankly, "are an ugly stubby toad." He fixed his hat and then climbed behind the wheel and started the truck without looking at her.

Chapter 13

Wyatt's blood was boiling. He was mad at the creep Brian. He was mad at Brian's deceptively named mother. He was mad at himself for suddenly being caught up in such an embarrassing drama. And he was also mad at the lovely Olivia—for kissing him in the middle of a Jerry Springer episode.

"I'm sorry," she mumbled after he'd put several miles between her and her ex-almost-mother-in-law.

He didn't know what to say to that. "Don't worry about it." He didn't want her to worry about it. He didn't want her to feel bad. He just wanted her out of his truck. He wanted this day over. He wanted to wake up the next morning and get back to work. That was what made him happy. How he'd gotten caught up in this domestic chaos he wasn't quite sure.

"How am I supposed to not worry?" she said after a minute. "You're a saint, and you're obviously mad at me. I didn't mean to do it. I didn't even think. I was just so emotionally over—"

He didn't want to hear her excuses. "I said don't worry about it. Let's pretend it never happened."

"That's not what you're doing!" she cried.

No, no it wasn't. He sighed. "I'm fine." Too late it struck him that this was a weird thing to say since she hadn't asked him how he was. He heard her sniffle, and his stomach rolled. A lot of people had made her cry lately, and he didn't need to pile on. "It's really okay, Olivia. I'm not mad. I'm not anything. I just got a little miffed because I don't like being used."

He heard her breath hitch, but she didn't say anything.

"There was a reason I wasn't in drama club back in school. I don't like being part of the show."

"What are you talking about?" Her voice was low, guttural.

He looked at her, tightening his grip on the wheel. "I thought I was being pretty clear. I didn't like being kissed as a way of ..." He didn't know how to finish that sentence. Maybe he wasn't being as clear as he thought. "I just don't like being used. I don't know how else to put it."

"I wasn't using you!" she cried.

He didn't want to be having this conversation. "Fine."

"Pull over."

"What?" He glanced at her.

"Please pull over."

It was like a drama avalanche chasing him down a mountain. "Why?"

"Pull over!" she nearly shrieked.

He pulled onto the shoulder and put the truck in park. What was she thinking? Where was she going to go? They were in the middle of nowhere. She stared at him, her eyes blazing. "I didn't use you," she said slowly.

Her gaze was unnerving, but he couldn't look away.

"You think I kissed you to make them mad or something?"

He wasn't quite sure. "Or something."

She groaned and rolled her eyes. "You're an idiot."

"I beg your pardon?" Maybe she could walk back to West Hope. It was only another ten miles or so.

She narrowed her eyes. "I don't care anything about what they think, and my brain doesn't work like that. I don't use people. I don't scheme and manipulate. I know you don't know me, but believe me when I say that. I have a lot of flaws, but I'm not an awful person." She sucked in some air. "You are like this gorgeous knight in shining armor. You swoop in and save me, and that back there?" She stabbed her thumb back over her shoulder. "That was like the worst moment of my entire life, and you were there, and you were just so wonderful, and I didn't mean to kiss you, and I'm sorry, and I probably shouldn't have, and I'm sorry"—her words spilled out faster and faster, practically crashing into each other as they fell— "but I didn't do it with some agenda. I did it because I'm an emotional mess and I lost control of myself for a second." She gasped for air, folded her arms across her chest, and then threw her upper body back into the seat like a toddler.

He didn't know what to do, so he laughed.

"Don't laugh at me," she said without looking at him. Her chin jutted out in defiance.

He laughed again. Then he looked at the road ahead of them and took a deep breath. "I apologize for real. I shouldn't have assumed you were being all Machiavellian."

"I don't know what that means."

"I'm not sure I do either." He reached for the box of chocolates on the dashboard. "Here, have some more Chubby Chipmunk, and let's call it a truce."

Chapter 14

"Why did he bring her back?" Chase Honeywood stood at the window looking out at his yard, which Wyatt had just pulled into with his branded contractor truck and his runaway bride. At least she wasn't wearing his sweatpants anymore. She looked like a normal person now. But still—he couldn't believe Wyatt had brought her back.

"What do you mean?" Hudson asked from the couch. "What did you think he was going to do with her? They were only going to get her things."

Chase hadn't known that. He hadn't known anything about the plan. He worked to be invisible, and usually it worked. People didn't go out of their way to fill him in on things. But Wyatt had driven off with her, so Chase had assumed he was taking her home, wherever that was.

"Look on the bright side," Hudson said. "Maybe Wyatt will make supper."

Chase doubted it. He was too busy making googoo gaga eyes at the prancing bride.

They made an awful lot of noise when they spilled in through the front door. Like two teenagers in love. It made his teeth ache. Not that he begrudged people being in love. He didn't. Just not in his house, within his earshot. He wanted to disappear, but he was hungry, and it was his turn to make supper.

Hudson was reading his mind as usual. "Wyatt, the least you could do for turning this into a bed and breakfast is make supper for everyone. There's some turkey burger in the fridge."

Chase almost gagged. Maybe he should make supper to protect himself from turkey burger. Hudson had convinced himself that the strangest things were healthy—tofu, bran muffins, and turkey everything. He'd even once defiled their home with turkey bacon, and Chase had threatened to move out and default on his share of the mortgage.

Hudson had promised no more turkey bacon, but Chase didn't really trust him.

"I'll cook supper!" the scorned bride squealed with excessive delight.

Her offer hung in the air; none of the brothers knew what to do with it.

"She's a professional cook," Wyatt said with a pride that didn't make sense. If she was a pro cook, what did that have to do with him? And weren't pro cooks called chefs?

"I don't care who cooks, as long as they don't make turkey."

Olivia beamed. "Great. I'll get started. You men relax." She and Wyatt exchanged a look that Chase couldn't quite interpret. One thing was for sure. This was really happening. His brother didn't just have a crush on the mystery woman. The attraction was mutual, and it was developing.

Good. Good for Wyatt. While Chase didn't think it was safe to go after a woman he knew nothing about, he knew Wyatt could handle himself. He had a good head on his shoulders. Chase went outside to put the horses in their stalls. The sun was sinking fast toward the horizon, shooting infinite layers of gold across the sky. Chase loved South Dakota so much that sometimes it made his chest ache.

He'd grown up wanting to leave. He'd found it boring, redundant, and painfully slow. Oh what a mistake he'd made. Not that he regretted it. He didn't. He'd done good things in the service, and he was glad he'd sacrificed for the freedom of others. But he'd been so wrong about leaving his home. It hadn't brought him the freedom he'd hoped, but it had made him appreciate what he had here, and now he would never, ever take it for granted again.

He hoped Wyatt's new friend would want to settle down close by. He would hate for his brother to move away. Not only would he miss him, but he knew Wyatt would miss South Dakota, even if he ended up somewhere almost as good.

His favorite mare nickered as he approached, and he ran a hand down her nose before he hooked the lead to her bridle. "I know, I know, Coffee. Strange things are afoot, but don't you worry. Our plan stays the same. One foot in front of the other, just like always."

He led her as he spoke softly, and he felt himself relax more with every step.

Chapter 15

Olivia was quite pleased with herself. The men had fallen silent as they enjoyed their food. She could sense Hudson's surprise. He hadn't expected it to taste as good as it did. She couldn't read Chase, but Wyatt was an open book—he was proud of her, and this made her feel like a million bucks. She didn't know what was going to happen with Wyatt, but the crazy notion that he liked her was growing less and less crazy in her mind.

If she'd been ten years younger, this wouldn't have been so hard to believe in the first place. She'd been quite the catch once upon a time.

Maybe she still was.

Hudson pushed his plate away. "Where did you say you used to cook?"

"The Cattlemen's Steakhouse." This embarrassed her a little. It was a good restaurant with a good reputation, but it wasn't exactly fine dining.

"In Spearfish?" Hudson said.

She nodded.

"Yeah," he said slowly, thoughtfully, as his eyes rolled up to look at his ceiling. "I ate there once years ago. I remember it was good." His eyes returned to hers. "Were you there a few years ago?"

She nodded. "I was there a long time." And never got a pay raise. Or a thank you.

"So interesting," Hudson said. "Small world. But you are a very good cook. Wyatt mentioned you won't be returning to Cattlemen's?"

She really hoped she wouldn't have to. "I think they might take me back if I groveled a bit, but I don't want to go back. Not that they were best friends with Brian or anything, sorry, he's the ex—"

Chase made a weird choking sound and reached for his water.

"—but I'd like to avoid the entire town if I can manage." She paused. "Not that it's a bad town or anything. It's not."

Hudson looked at Wyatt. "I must know someone in the restaurant business in West Hope."

"If you don't know them, then you've at least stitched them up at some point," Wyatt said.

Hudson chuckled. "Yeah, maybe. Or at least I've stitched up their kid."

"Might be time to call in a favor," Wyatt said.

Hudson looked at her again. "I absolutely will if I can think of a good person to reach out to. Give me a minute to flip through the people I know. There are a lot of them."

"She could cook here," Wyatt said, and Olivia nearly jumped in her chair. Sure, the thought had crossed her mind, but she wasn't going to say it out loud.

Hudson chuckled. "I hardly think we can afford a full-time cook, and she's not going to work for free."

"You should have seen this place she was going to have her wedding. It wasn't exactly in shambles, but it's probably not going to make the cover of any magazines anytime soon either."

Chase leaned back in his chair, his expression darkening with suspicion.

Olivia wished Wyatt would stop talking. This wasn't helping her case any.

"Maybe she could go cook at the Bannon Ranch. Mrs. Bannon might like to retire."

Wyatt scoffed, "I don't think that woman will ever give up the spatula."

"What kind of place was this wedding going to be at?" Hudson took out his phone.

Wyatt rattled off the name and address. "It looks like a giant house. It had an okay view of the hills, but that was its only selling point as far as I could tell."

"The food was good," Olivia mumbled, but everyone ignored her.

"You were going to get married in a house?" Hudson was frowning down at his phone.

"Well, yeah, but it's an event center. Like that's what they do. People pay to have events there. Parties, maybe small conferences."

"Oh! Yeah! I know this place." Hudson scrolled. "Years ago it was like a hippie artist colony."

Chase made the choking sound again.

"Then the artists had a falling out and sold it." He looked up. "So now it's a wedding venue? Interesting." He looked down again and scrolled some more. "The pictures look pretty good."

"The pictures are deceiving," Wyatt said. "They've been touched up a bit. The place needs some work. I was going to leave my card until Olivia broke in. Then I didn't really want them to know I'd been there."

"You broke in?" Hudson cried, suddenly worried he was harboring a fugitive.

For the first time, Chase looked interested in the conversation.

"I didn't *break* in," Olivia said.

"What would you call it? You went in through a window!"

"But I didn't steal anything. I just got my stuff."

Chase continued to stare at her, looking oddly impressed. It almost seemed a smile was tickling his mouth, trying to break through. What an odd group of brothers this was. They couldn't be more different, and she'd been hanging out with the most normal one. She was grateful Wyatt was the one who'd staggered out in the dark to investigate her loud arrival.

"But you went in through a window?" Hudson said again, clearly horrified.

"I did. Desperate times and all that." She studied the tabletop.

"Anyway," Wyatt said, "my point is that maybe you could do events here."

Chase let out a strangled groan.

"Not all the time. Just a few in the summer to help offset costs. This place is clearly looking nicer than that place—"

Chase pushed his chair back suddenly; he didn't say anything, but the loud scraping sound said it all. He turned and headed outside, leaving his chair pushed back and his empty plate on the table.

"Sorry," Wyatt said. "Wasn't trying to make him mad, but it would help pay for his breeding program. You know, till it gets off the ground. And Olivia could cook for the events."

Hudson was staring at her.

"This isn't my idea," she said weakly, though it sort of was. But she wasn't stupid enough to bring it up at the table. In front of Chase.

"No, it's my idea, and it's a good one."

"She still needs a real job, Wyatt," Hudson said. He wasn't wrong. "And I don't think this small ranch is going to attract many hopeful brides. We're not in the Black Hills." He said it as if it were the final word.

"Fine." Wyatt stood up and reached across the table for Chase's plate. "I'll do the dishes."

"I'll help." She jumped up, glad for something to do.

Chapter 16

"I'm sorry," Wyatt said as he handed Olivia a plate to dry. "It was just an idea. I don't know why everyone's so annoyed." All his life, he'd been able to see money-making opportunities so clearly, it was as if they were written in words floating in the air. This was one of them—no matter what his brothers thought.

Olivia didn't say anything, further souring his mood.

"But I wasn't volunteering you for the job so much as brainstorming."

"I know that," she said softly. Her voice really was lovely, even when he was in a bad mood. "And they know that too. I think Hudson was resistant just as a way to protect Chase. And I have no idea why Chase was so resistant, other than the fact that he hates me."

"He doesn't hate you," Wyatt hurried to say. "I promise you. He doesn't hate anyone." He took a deep breath. "Chase has suffered from PTSD. He hasn't had an incident in a long time, but I don't know if that's because he's been cured or because he stays away from anything that might trigger him. But when he first got home from the service, it was really bad. In fact, he knew it was bad before he ever got home. He let Hudson know way in advance that he was going to need help."

"Wow. I'm so sorry. I shouldn't have made a snap judgment."

"No worries. I can see why people would think he is a grumpy jerk, but he's not. He's never been a jerk. He just *really* doesn't like crowds of people, so when I said the word event, he panicked. In fact, now that I think about it, I really shouldn't have used that word. But I wasn't thinking." No, that wasn't quite right. "Well, I was thinking, but I was thinking about you and about his horse program, which really is a good idea, but it's just been so slow getting it started. I know the financial part is causing them both stress. Well, maybe not Chase, but I know it's causing Hudson some stress."

"I'm surprised they can afford to fix the place up then."

"You mean what I'm doing?"

She nodded and took another dripping plate from his hand.

"Yeah, they're not paying for that. I'm just helping out in my spare time."

"Wow." She sounded impressed.

"It's really not that big of a deal. They're my brothers."

"So what are you fixing up, exactly?"

She was right. There wasn't much evidence. Yet.

"The layout of the barn wasn't working for Chase, so I'm remodeling there. And just trying to make the whole place look better.

If someone comes to look at a horse, we want the place to look professional, not destitute."

"It doesn't look destitute. Not even close." She chuckled dryly. "Well, maybe the hole in the front barn looks a bit destitute, but I'll be paying for that soon. You won't have to fix it pro bono."

He laughed and handed her the last plate. "I'm no lawyer."

"Sorry. I'm not sure what to call it when a contractor works for free."

"Yeah, me neither." He peeked into the living room, which was blessedly empty. "I'm going to go soon, but I'd like to put my feet up for a few minutes first." This was kind of a lie. He wasn't the least bit tired. He just wasn't ready to leave her yet.

"So no one's actually invited me to stay for another night." She giggled uncomfortably. "Are you sure it's okay with Hudson?"

"Oh, absolutely. Don't worry. He'd make it clear to me if he wanted you out. But he's not like that. You'd have to be really obnoxious for him to be inhospitable."

"Good to know." She followed him into the living room and sat in a recliner, which was a little disappointing. He'd hoped she'd sit on the couch with him.

"So I'm sad to say that I have to get back to my real work tomorrow. This weekend has been fun, but I have deadlines."

"I figured as much. I wish I knew of a way to make myself useful tomorrow. I need to do something other than wait. I'm waiting for Rodney to fix my truck, and I'm waiting for the insurance guy to come on Wednesday. Though, I've pretty much decided to stay in the area, so maybe I should officially start my job hunt."

"Going to be hard to do without a vehicle."

"Yep, and they left my laptop out in the rain, so not even sure that will turn on."

"Hey, you should put it in a bag of rice. I know Hudson has some zipper baggies around here somewhere as well as rice. Very brown and very organic, but still rice."

"Zipper baggies big enough for a laptop?"

"Good point. You might need two. And some duct tape."

She sighed. "Okay. Thank you. Organic rice, huh? I hear the organic stuff absorbs more water."

He chuckled. "You should test that theory out before you go to bed. And as far as a vehicle, you can use mine."

"Seriously?" Her shock was palpable.

"Uh, yeah. It's a truck, not a time machine. Of course you can use it."

She giggled. "Thank you. That's very generous. I'm surprised you're not making certain assumptions about my driving skills."

He laughed heartily. That hadn't even occurred to him. "Don't thank me yet." He studied her in the soft light from the television. She was gorgeous. He wished she wasn't sitting so far away. "You'd have to get up pretty early. I can pick you up on the way to the job site, and then we can drop me off, and you can do whatever you need to do. Just don't forget to pick me back up."

"Is this ranch on the way to the job site?"

"Not even close."

She groaned.

Had she not figured out yet that he would gladly drive her to the ends of the earth? "It's fine. Trust me. I'll pick you up bright and early." He sighed. He should get some sleep. This adrenaline rush was going to wear off eventually. He sighed and stood up. "Which means I should go home and get some shuteye."

"Do you know of any landlords who take credit cards?"

He looked down at her, not understanding.

"I don't have much money in savings right now thanks to the wedding, but I'd like to look for a place. I just need to find one that takes credit."

"Sorry. I don't know any landlords period, let alone one who takes credit, but I can ask around." He wished she would just stay at the ranch for a while, but he could see how that might not be her first choice. And it definitely wasn't Chase's first choice. "Okay, then. Good night. Don't forget about the rice."

She smiled up at him, and it nearly took his breath away. "I won't. Don't forget about me between now and tomorrow morning."

"Not a chance," he said and headed for the door.

Chapter 17

It was a trip driving Wyatt's truck. Olivia felt a bit giddy, a bit powerful, a bit rebellious. She wasn't even sure why she was enjoying it so much, but she certainly was. She was reluctant to get out of the truck to go into businesses and ask about work, but getting back into the truck brought the rush all over again. It smelled like Wyatt. It *felt* like Wyatt. *Whoa, girl.* She tried to slow herself down. If you're going to fall in love with him, it needs to be a slow, controlled, rational fall—not that head over heels stuff from the movies.

Firstly, she had to protect her heart. Wyatt might be out of her league, which meant he could do her heart some serious damage. And secondly, she had to make sure he really was as awesome as he seemed. She didn't have time to waste on getting tangled up with another toad, even one that wasn't stubby.

She visited three restaurants before she ran out of verve for that particular flavor of rejection. Each of the people she spoke to were kind, but they had all the cooks they needed. The third one, however, told her that the county jail was desperate for cooks. She had never had a particular desire to work at a jail, but she needed a job, and it was a county job, so he'd even used the word *benefits*. This excited her greatly. She'd never had a job with benefits before.

She used her phone to apply for the jail job online. While she was on the county website, she saw that the library was also hiring. They probably wouldn't let her cook anything there, but she couldn't imagine a more peaceful job than a library gig—and it would certainly give her easy access to the cookbook section. So she applied for that job too.

Then she kept driving and thinking. A chain pizza restaurant was hiring, but she wasn't sure that would be a good idea. She had a feeling they wouldn't let her tinker with the recipes, and she'd likely gain a hundred pounds while she worked there. She saw a sign for a receptionist and filled out an application, secretly hoping that they wouldn't want her but not in any position to be choosy. She was standing in the grocery store staring at a flyer stuck on a bulletin board—Sanitary Truck Workers Wanted! Great pay! —when her phone buzzed. She hurried to answer and then headed toward the corner of the store in hopes of cutting down on the elevator music.

It didn't work. Apparently there was a speaker in the corner of the store. She pressed her hand to her free ear so she could hear better. It was the jail asking her to come in for an interview. Seriously? Right now? She told them that she was in town but that she wasn't dressed for an interview. She didn't add that she couldn't get dressed for an interview without doing some quick shopping. But they told her not to worry, that she should come in right away. Good grief, they sounded desperate.

Perfect.

She told them she'd be right there.

The jail didn't provide a very welcoming atmosphere—no surprise there—but the uniformed woman who greeted her was friendly and showed her to the administrative offices, which were only slightly more inviting. A frazzled-looking woman in a blazer and blue jeans came around a cluttered desk to shake her hand and introduce herself. Then Lexi offered Olivia a seat.

Olivia could tell she was going to get hired unless she did something really awful in the next twenty minutes. This knowledge allowed her to relax and be herself.

"You know, I don't want to look a gift horse in the mouth, but you're a bit overqualified."

Olivia smiled. "Maybe, but I need a reliable job, and I heard the word *benefits*."

Lexi laughed and dug through a tall stack of folders till she found the one she wanted, which she handed across the desk. "Here are your benefits. Since it's only a part-time job, there are only partial benefits, but that's still better than not having any."

This was the first time Olivia had heard the word part-time, but Lexi made a good point. Olivia thanked her and promised to look it over.

"Sounds good. Can you start Wednesday?"

She could start right now, but sure, she'd wait till Wednesday. "Absolutely. Thank you for the opportunity."

"You're welcome. And just so you know, these part-time jobs often turn full-time before long."

Olivia nodded. "Okay."

Lexi narrowed her eyes. "May I ask, do you have any leads on any other good jobs? I don't want to get too excited if you're just going to get a better offer tomorrow."

Olivia couldn't tell if she was joking. "Uh ... the only other thing I've seen that looked interesting was the library, and I'm pretty sure that's only on Saturdays." As she spoke, Lexi grew visibly excited. "Hey, my sister is the librarian there! Would you like me to make a phone call?"

"Uh ... sure."

By the time Olivia was headed back to Wyatt's job site, she had two job offers, and she couldn't have been more excited.

But Wyatt's excitement did not match her own. In fact, it was quite the opposite.

Chapter 18

"The county jail?" Wyatt cried. He must have heard her wrong. As much talent as Olivia had? As much restaurant experience? And that's what she ended up with? The county jail? Cooking for criminals?

"They offer benefits."

She'd already said that twice, and benefits were a good thing, but it was still a *jail*. And he'd heard horror stories about that jail. People from his church used to go there to lead Bible studies, and the jail had made them take a hiatus. So far, the hiatus had lasted two years. A fight had broken out, and one of the volunteers had tried to break it up and had gotten seriously hurt. Wyatt couldn't imagine sending a pregnant woman into that environment. "You have no training. What if someone tries to hurt you?" He couldn't stop himself from glancing at her stomach. "It's just not safe. Please, think about all the factors involved."

"Factors?" she cried. "The *factors* are so simple. I need a job. This is a job. A job with *benefits*."

When was she going to just come out and tell him that she was pregnant? If she didn't do it soon, he was going to have to say something. This was ridiculous. Especially if they were going to have a relationship. What was she waiting for? Did she think he wasn't going to notice when her belly kept growing and then a baby popped out?

He took a steadying breath and stepped closer. He didn't want to be mad at her. "I'm sorry, okay? I'm not trying to be a brute."

"I wasn't thinking that you were a brute."

"Good. I'm just worried about you. Hey, I'm almost done here. Give me a minute, and then I'll give you a ride back to the ranch. I bet they'd let you cook for us again, if you're up for it?"

This made her smile. "I'm always up for cooking."

"Good. If you want, we can even stop at the grocery store and get you some supplies. Then you don't have to be limited by Hudson's weird pantry offerings."

Her eyes lit up. "That would be great! Would you text them and tell them I'm cooking? I'll go make a list." Having forgotten all about him, she spun toward the truck.

He texted Hudson right away so that he wouldn't forget. Then he finished picking up; as he did so, he tried to sort his thoughts. He really had to stop thinking like this was the beginning of a relationship. It *wasn't*, not until he got the details on this pregnancy. If some other man was out there wanting to be a father—even if that man was the awful Brian—then maybe Wyatt wasn't supposed to be with her. He didn't like this thought one bit, but he wanted to do the right thing.

On his way back to the truck, a new thought hit him, and it was so obvious that he felt like a complete dunce.

The *benefits*.

That meant health insurance.

He almost smacked himself in the forehead. *Of course*. He'd been thinking that she was taking this job without thinking of the baby, but she was probably taking this job *because* she was thinking of the baby. How could he have been so stupid?

He still didn't like the idea of her working at the jail, but he finally understood her motivation. Sure, she could work at a restaurant and maybe get a little bit of glory—or she could work at a jail and get health insurance. It all made sense now.

He climbed into the truck intent on apologizing.

"How does steak enchilada casserole sound?" She sounded excited.

His stomach roared to life. "It sounds heavenly."

"Did Hudson answer you?"

He checked his phone. "No, not yet, but that doesn't mean anything. He's probably still at work. I promise, they're going to let you cook." *And even if they don't, I'll let you cook for me*, he silently added. "So I was thinking about it, and I'm sorry I got so shook up. I can see why the jail job is attractive to you. I just ... I want you to be safe."

"No, you're right, and I'm sorry."

He was? She was? "Really?"

"Yeah. I get it. A lot can happen at a jail. I see your point."

Oh wow. That was good then, right? It was settled.

He drove her to the grocery store, followed her around while she tried to be choosy in a store without many choices, and then drove her to the ranch—where Chase had already started cooking. Wyatt groaned.

He was an idiot for promising. He pulled her aside. "I'm so sorry," he whispered. "I've never seen him do this before." Granted, Wyatt wasn't usually at the ranch for supper, so maybe Chase did this all the time, but he really hadn't thought that was the case.

He could tell she was disappointed, but she was also gracious. "No worries, really."

He helped her put her supplies in the fridge, and Chase glanced at them suspiciously. "You guys are making me nervous with all your hovering. Why don't you go watch television or something."

They were hardly hovering. They hadn't even been there for five minutes. But Olivia seemed in as much of a hurry to get away from Chase as he was to be rid of her. She practically scampered into the living room, and this time, she sat on the couch.

Good. They were making progress then.

Wyatt sat beside her—not too close, though. He wasn't sure if this was going to be a thing, so he didn't want to act like it was, even if his heart was desperately trying to head in that direction.

"What do you want to watch?" she asked.

"You pick."

"If I pick, it's going to be a cooking show."

"That works for me." Wyatt was pretty sure he'd never watched a cooking show, but it was a good day for new things. He'd never fallen in love with a pregnant woman before either.

About two minutes after Hudson walked through the door, Chase announced that supper was ready. Wyatt hadn't officially been invited yet, so he asked if there was enough for him. Chase grunted a reply that Wyatt interpreted as affirmative.

He pulled out Olivia's chair for her, and Hudson hid a smile while Chase didn't hide his grimace. As soon as he had Olivia convinced she wanted to spend the rest of her life with him, he was going to get right to work finding Chase a woman. Someone needed to cheer this guy up.

The ham was cold and as tough as leather. The potatoes were raw in the middle. And Wyatt couldn't identify what was wrong with the peas, but something was very, very wrong with the peas. They all ate in silence, and there was a lot of water guzzling as they each tried to wash down the atrocities that were Chase's meal.

Everyone knew what everyone else was thinking, but no one said anything.

Until Olivia said, "If you guys want, I could cook supper tomorrow."

Though Chase didn't so much as flinch, Wyatt could sense his rage, so he quickly said, "Let's go for a walk, Olivia!" He stood up quickly.

She looked surprised, but she agreed. She took care of her plate first, though, and then thanked Chase on her way by.

Wyatt took her elbow and gently rushed her outside.

"What's wrong?" she said, her innocence so precious.

"Oh nothing. I just really wanted to get you alone." He nearly yelped at his own stupidity. Had he really just said that aloud? "Sorry, I just mean that my brothers really annoy me sometimes." This wasn't even true. *Good grief, Wyatt, stop talking.*

They walked to the nearest fence and then leaned on it.

"I mean, just look at this place," she said dreamily. "I get it, why Chase doesn't want people here, especially wedding parties. They're the most stressed-out parties of all, which makes them the most obnoxious, but look at this place. It's so pastoral, so picturesque. The butte in the background, and this perfect creek winding its way through the land. How can you not see it?"

"I do see it, but it's not my ranch."

She eyed him. "But can't you sell it to him?"

Sell what to who? His brothers had already bought it. "I'm sorry?"

"Sell Hudson on the idea. I mean, I have no skin in the game, but if they're having money troubles, I think this is their answer."

"They're not having money troubles. Chase's dream just isn't growing as fast as they'd hoped. Or as fast as Hudson hoped, anyway. I don't know what Chase is hoping for. I think he's just happy with the horses he has." Chase had no interest in money, it seemed.

"Okay." She held onto the fence and leaned her body back. Her hair fell behind her, and it was all he could do not to reach up and run his fingers through it.

Chapter 19

Hudson sat at the kitchen table, his eyes bouncing between the clock on the wall and the closed door of the guest bedroom. Last night Wyatt had shared Olivia's vision for the ranch with him, and he really wanted to pick her brain before going to work, but he also had to get going or he was going to be behind schedule all day.

Finally, her door opened, and he popped up to pour her some coffee. "Good morning!" he said brightly. He handed her the mug.

"Thanks." She eyed him with suspicion.

"You're welcome. Hey, Wyatt told me about your thoughts about hosting events here. Mind if I ask you a few questions?"

She nervously glanced toward Chase's bedroom door.

"Don't worry. He's outside."

"Oh. Okay, then. Sure." She pulled out a chair and sat.

"So, can you give me an overview?"

She took a long drink of her coffee, and he felt bad for assaulting her first thing in the morning.

She was a good sport, though, and gave him the rundown, saying essentially the same thing Wyatt had said the night before, some parts of it word for word. "It wouldn't have to be every weekend. You could just do a few events. I'm telling you, people would pay for it. They'd pay a pretty penny."

"How much are we talking? I checked out some other places in the state, but none of their websites listed a dollar amount."

"That's 'cause the dollar amount is so high." She chuckled and drank some more coffee, while he tried to be patient.

It was a good thing that he'd finished his coffee, or he would've choked on it when she finally told him what she'd spent on the Black Hills joint. "You're kidding," he said when he'd regained his bearings.

"Oh believe me, I wish I was. I paid for that whole kit and caboodle. Even had to pay for his sister's bridesmaid dress because she couldn't afford it." Her fingers made air quotes around the last few words, and Hudson felt bad for making her relive her near-wedding trauma.

He could not believe that price tag. He could buy a good used truck for that cost. Or even better, Chase could buy a great mare with that price tag. How could Chase not think that was worth it? A single weekend with a ranch full of strangers would be terrible for him—*but* he'd get to pick out a new mare.

"What would we need to offer them?"

She looked contemplative. "Best case scenario would include lodging. You'd probably want to get a liquor license. And you'd need an indoor event hall and an outdoor shelter of some sort, though that could be a tent, though the tents are pretty expensive too—"

Hudson held up a hand. "Whoa, whoa." Maybe he should be taking notes. "Lodging? Like they would sleep here?"

"Well, they don't need to, but there's no hotel nearby, and most people will be drinking. You can charge them a lot more if you let them sleep here."

Interesting. "Okay, and then the liquor license makes sense. So how big does the event hall need to be, you think?"

"About the size of the barn I tried to destroy." Her eyes fell.

"Wyatt said it wouldn't be too difficult to repair that. Don't you worry about that. So ..." He couldn't believe that the answer to what he was about to ask could be yes, but he couldn't believe anything so far, so ... "You think that the front barn would be big enough? And good enough if we fixed it up?"

She nodded readily. "You wouldn't even have to fix it up much. People want that rustic barn look."

People were so, so weird. "What else do we need?"

"Parking. I don't know if zoning would be an issue?"

She was a smart cookie. "In West Hope? I don't think so."

"Plumbing might be tough. Might need to get some water storage and get some delivery set up, but it wouldn't take long to pay for that once the bookings start. And of course, you should offer them a sweet catering package." She leaned back and gave him a dramatic smile. Her coffee was kicking in. "Might be some code issues too. I don't know how any of that works, but if we have people sleeping here, we probably need to have a certain amount of outlets and smoke alarms, I would imagine."

It was adorable that she kept saying *we*.

"But I'm sure Wyatt can get things up to code no problem."

There was a sparkle in her eye when she said Wyatt's name. Hudson decided something in that moment. He decided that, despite the fact that this woman had fled her wedding, momentarily lost her mind, and driven into the side of his barn in the middle of the night, he really liked her. He also decided that he wanted his brother Wyatt to end up with her. He had never considered himself a matchmaker, but for the first time he wondered how he could help push two people together.

Turning his ranch into a wedding venue might be a good start.

"Thanks so much, Olivia. I need to talk to Chase."

"Good luck," she said, and he tried to ignore the doubt in her voice. Chase was anti-social, but he wasn't an idiot. He was going to see the logic behind this. Hudson just had to show it to him.

Chapter 20

"Not you too," Chase said. He couldn't believe this was happening. This woman was infecting his brothers, one at a time. "Want me to call Seth and Dustin, get them over here so you can all gang up on me? I might even be able to find Burke if I really work at it."

"When I tell those guys, they're going to see the value in this idea." Hudson was being very patient, and Chase was grateful, but Chase really, really didn't want to do this.

"Hudson, man, this was supposed to be my sanctuary."

"And it still will be. It's going to be a sanctuary with a lot more horses. Look, these people won't be here every day. It will only be on—"

"But they *will* be here. What am I supposed to do while they're here?"

"You don't have to do anything! You can stay in the house."

Chase managed to not growl, but he was pretty sure Hudson felt his fury.

"That's not what I meant. I didn't mean you had to hide, or that you'd want to stay inside. I just meant that you don't have to help with this in any way. You can just reap the benefits."

"So who's going to do it? You, Doctor? In all your spare time?"

"I don't know who is going to do what. I don't think we need to figure that out until we decide it's going to happen."

He was definitely putting the cart before the horse, then. "*We?* So I still have a say in all this?"

"Of course you do," Hudson said quickly. "I'm not trying to strong-arm you into anything. I just want you to see the potential here." He threw some numbers at him, but Chase didn't even try to process them. "That's a lot of horses."

Chase sighed. He could see Hudson's point. His little breeding program wasn't exactly taking off like wildfire. He'd sold one foal and added one mare in two years. He knew that he was in the red. He'd been paying his bills out of his savings. "Can I think about it?"

"Of course. Take your time." Hudson started to go.

"I'm sorry," he said, and he meant it. "But I ... I can't imagine having that many people here." He scanned the landscape, his beloved, holy landscape. "I mean, all those *people*. All that noise." He looked at his oldest brother. "Can you really picture that? And if you can, it seems like a good thing?"

Hudson stepped closer. "It seems like a *neutral* thing. A thing that could help us. But I really don't want to do it if you're not on board, okay?"

Chase nodded. "Okay." He watched his brother walk away.

Yes, he would think about this. He would pray about it. But he didn't think he would ever be able to get on board.

Chapter 21

Olivia was going a bit stir crazy. For years, she'd worked herself to exhaustion, slept, and then gone back to work. Then she'd stopped working in order to frantically prepare for a wedding. And then she'd had a few days of adrenaline-fueled chaos.

But all of that was over now, and now she was just waiting—waiting for Wednesday so she could go to her new job and start over again.

She couldn't stand sitting around, and she wanted to avoid Chase, so she wandered into the barn that might soon be a big, fancy event hall. Of course, first they had to deal with the giant gaping hole in the wall. She stood there with her hands on her hips staring at it. She couldn't believe that she'd done that. Couldn't believe that she'd exhausted herself to the point of falling asleep at the wheel.

It was a really good thing that there'd been a barn in the way to break her fall. A barn, and the handsomest, sweetest carpenter slash cowboy on the planet. She silently thanked God that he'd allowed her to smash into this particular barn. Of all the barns in South Dakota, he'd picked the best possible one.

But right now, this barn was a mess. She didn't have a pickup bed or a dumpster, but she could at least start dragging some of the debris outside and pile it up. Then when she got her truck back, she could haul it off. Or maybe Chase would help her start a big old bonfire. That seemed like the kind of thing he might enjoy.

She went back into the house and snooped around until she found an old pair of gloves, and then she headed back outside.

It felt good to work. Her blood started flowing, she started sweating a little in the sweet warmth of spring, and she was really enjoying herself—until she heard a man shout, "Stop!"

She straightened and whirled around to find Wyatt standing in the doorway. Wow, he was home already? She hadn't realized how much time had gone by.

"What are you doing?" he cried. His tone made it sound like he'd caught her kicking kittens.

"I got bored, so I thought I'd pick up a little."

He stomped toward her. "You did all this by yourself?"

She couldn't tell if he was impressed or furious. Was it possible to be both at the same time? "Uh, yeah. But I've been at it for—"

He grabbed her arm and gently pulled her into a beam of light. Then he looked her up and down. "Olivia, you shouldn't be doing this!"

"Wyatt, if you're worried about me making it look better before the insurance guy gets here, I haven't even touched that wall. I've just been picking up inside the barn."

"I'm not worried about that. It's just that you shouldn't be doing all this heavy lifting when you're—" He stopped abruptly.

"When I'm what?"

He stepped back, letting go of her arm. "You know."

No, she didn't know. She put her hands on her hips. "When I'm what?" What did he think she was, some fragile doll? "What is wrong with you?"

"It's not good for ... I just ..." He whirled around. "Never mind!" He stomped off like a toddler, but then he stopped before he got to the door and turned back. "I'm sorry. I don't mean to be bossy. I just don't want you to hurt yourself."

She stared at him. One might assume that a man like this had an even keel, but she was realizing that this wasn't the case. This was the same nuttiness he'd revealed when she'd told him about the jail job. She sighed. Since he was already in a bad mood, it might be a good time to ask him for a ride. She started toward the door. "I won't hurt myself. I promise. Let me make you that supper I promised you. Oh, and could you give me a ride to my new job tomorrow?"

He stopped walking, turned, and stared at her. "What new job?"

Okay, she needed to stop falling for this guy. Some days, sure, he was perfect. But on other days, he was a complete wacko. "The jail job."

"The jail job?" he cried. He took a step back.

She stared at him, unsure what to say. Hadn't they already fought about this once? And why were they fighting about it at all? He had no say in what job she took or didn't take.

"The jail job?" he said again. "But you said you weren't going to take that job!"

"What?" She had said no such thing. Ever.

"You said that I was right, and that it was dangerous."

"Uh ... no." She couldn't remember what she'd said, exactly, but she hadn't said that she was going to turn the job down. That would have been stupid. She needed that job. How did he not get that?

"You know what." He looked down and ran a hand over his face. "I just need a minute. And yeah I'll give you a ride." He headed toward the house, keeping his head down, and she didn't know what to do.

She took off her work gloves and looked around. Maybe it was time she moved on. She needed to not get any further attached to this ranch. Or to anyone who spent time here.

Chapter 22

Wyatt felt bad about it, but he avoided the kitchen while Olivia was preparing supper. He didn't want to be mad at her. He definitely didn't want to fight with her. And he was really tired of having this giant secret between them. He liked her; she liked him back, he was pretty sure; so they had to discuss this third person in the equation.

"Trouble in paradise?" Hudson knocked Wyatt's feet off the coffee table and sat down beside him.

"I don't know."

"Yes, you do. What's going on?"

Wyatt groaned. "We're having trouble with communication."

"What? That doesn't sound like you. And I don't know her that well yet, but I don't get the impression that she's unable to communicate."

"Oh, she's able. She's just not willing."

"What does that mean? Is she unwilling to admit that she likes you? Because believe me, she does. I've seen it."

"You've seen it?" What did that mean?

"When she says your name, her whole face lights up." Hudson elbowed him. "Nice work, man."

Despite himself, Wyatt grinned.

"So even if she won't admit it, she likes you."

"That's not the problem. In fact, we're not even there yet."

"Not there yet? She's living in my house! What are you waiting for?"

Wyatt groaned. "Sorry."

"No, you don't need to be sorry. But now you're the one who's failing to communicate. Tell me what's going on. Maybe I can help."

"There's just some stuff going on in her life, and she needs to tell me. I mean, I already know, but she doesn't know that I know, so she needs to tell me so that we can both know that I know. And I do need to know ... before we can move onto the next step in forming any sort of relationship."

"Whoa, man. That's a lot."

"Yeah." Wyatt stared at the TV without seeing it.

"So, what's the thing she has to tell you?"

Wyatt looked at his big brother the doctor. How could he not know? How could he not see? Granted, it hadn't been so obvious once she'd taken of that tight, wet wedding dress, but still. That night it had been obvious enough. "It's not my secret to tell," he finally said, just before Olivia called from the kitchen that supper was ready.

She stared at him as he took his seat at the table, and he panicked at the thought that she'd overheard them talking. He didn't think she could have, but he hadn't exactly been whispering. He tried to smile at her, but she didn't return the favor.

When she finally sat down, he thanked her for cooking. She graciously said, "You're welcome" without looking at him.

Oh boy. What a mess he'd made. He ate his meal in silence, which was difficult because it was so delicious he really wanted to praise her. She truly was a talented cook. He couldn't imagine her wasting that talent reheating pre-prepared processed food from a tub so she could scoop it into trays. But she did need health insurance. And that's when it hit him.

How could he not have thought of it before? He had employees. And they all had health insurance.

He managed to hold his idea inside until they'd all finished eating. And he held it inside while he did the dishes. This time, she did not offer to help with the drying. She'd just gone straight for her room and shut the door.

When he'd gotten all the plates balanced on the drying rack, he knocked softly on her door and invited her to go for a walk. He half expected her to ignore the invitation, but the door opened, and she smiled up at him tentatively before stepping out of the room.

She didn't verbally accept his invitation, but she headed for the front door, so he inferred that she was willing. By the time they got outside and shut the door behind them, his idea practically exploded out of him: "Let me hire you to fix the barn."

She let out a weird sound that was part laugh, part anguished cry. "What?"

"I'm sorry I'm being such a jerk about the jail. And I'm sorry I didn't think of this sooner, but I have employees. So let me hire you. You'll get your health insurance."

She took a step back, slowly shaking her head.

"What? What's wrong?"

"This ... this feels like charity."

"It's not," he said quickly. "And it wouldn't be forever." *Just till the baby's born. Just till we can think of a better plan.* "It's just for now. Bridge the gap until you can find the cooking gig you really want."

"So you want to ..." She spoke the words slowly, carefully. "... pay me to fix the barn that I destroyed."

He tried to squelch his smile and failed. "Yeah, but don't put it like that."

"How would you like me to put it?"

"I saw that you got a lot of work done in one day. And I know you're smart. I have three job sites right now and if we're going to turn this place into a wedding venue—"

"Are we doing that?" she interrupted, sounding hopeful.

"Maybe. Hudson's still working on Chase."

Her face fell.

"But either way, we've got to get the barn fixed sooner rather than later. And I can afford to hire you to do that. So let me. It's a win-win."

She didn't look convinced. He stepped closer to her. He couldn't believe how strong his desire was to take care of her, to provide of her. "Please. Let me do this. It will make me happy. And then I don't have to worry about you at the jail."

"You don't have to worry about me at the jail either way."

"I know," he said quickly. "I'm not trying to control you. I'm not trying to micromanage you. I'm just ..."

"Just what?" She tilted her face up to his, and he desperately wanted to feel those lips on his own again. He hadn't allowed himself to enjoy it the first time, and he'd tried not to think about it since.

"I want to take care of you."

"That's really sweet of you," she said, her voice softer than he'd ever heard it.

"I can be sweet when I want to be."

She narrowed her eyes playfully. "You realize I have no idea how to build things."

"You can swing a hammer."

"I bet it's a bit more complicated than that."

It was. "I can teach you the rest." He couldn't take his eyes off her lips.

"Fine. I'll work for you. On one condition."

"What's that?"

"I'm keeping the library job."

He laughed. "Yeah. That would be okay, I think." He hadn't heard any scary stories about the library.

"Of course that's if they'll still have me. I'm about to royally tick off the librarian's sister when I don't show up for work with hardly any notice."

She was right, and that was totally his fault. "You know what? Let me take care of Lexi."

"You know Lexi?"

"This is West Hope. Everybody knows everybody."

Chapter 23

Olivia woke in a state of sheer terror. At first she'd thought she'd been having a nightmare, but then she heard the scream again.

A man's voice—shouting so loud that his voice cracked on every other word. His desperation shook the walls. Chase.

Chase was screaming. Screaming for someone named Palmer.

Olivia's whole body went cold, even though she was sweating. She had never heard someone sound that scared.

Should she do something?

A door shut, and then footfall thudded between Chase's cries. Hudson was on the scene. Good. She relaxed a little. He would do whatever could be done, though she doubted there was much. Wake him up, probably. Remind him that he was home in South Dakota, that he was safe. She hoped that Palmer, whoever he was, was also home safe.

But she had a feeling that he wasn't.

She prayed a long prayer then, first for Palmer and his family, and then for Chase. She said "amen," with a new realization: she needed to be nicer to Chase. Not that she'd been unkind thus far, but she hadn't really gone out of her way to be friendly either, which, now that she was thinking about it, was pretty ridiculous. She was staying in his house. And though he wasn't happy about it, he hadn't thrown her out either. He'd hardly put up a fight.

She tried to fall back asleep, but she felt like she'd just guzzled a Starbucks double shot. When she could manage to stop worrying about Chase, her mind went right to fantasizing about Wyatt: about what it would feel like to rest in his arms; about kissing him again and actually having him kiss her back; about all the wonderful meals she could cook for him. And when she tried to stop imagining a beautiful future with Wyatt, she went right back to grieving for Chase.

When the clock hit five o'clock, she figured she might as well just get up.

Her feet hit the floor, and she groaned. It felt like she hadn't slept at all. She got dressed and staggered out into the kitchen, startling when she saw Chase by the coffee pot. "Oh sorry, I didn't know you were up." She flinched. That hadn't made much sense. What, like she wouldn't have come out here if she'd known that he was there?

"No worries," he said softly. "Morning."

"Good morning. Want me to make you some breakfast?"

He hesitated, and she worried she'd offended him.

"Actually, yeah. I'll take you up on that, but I've got to do some stuff outside first. I'll be right back. And if you want to throw some extra eggs in the pan, Hudson will be up soon."

"No prob. I always make extra." She opened the fridge to see what she had to work with. If she was going to keep this up, they should let her do the grocery shopping too.

Chase had been right. Hudson soon appeared.

"I'm making breakfast." She tried to sound cheerful, but to her ears she only sounded tired.

"That's very kind of you."

She glanced at the door and then looked at Hudson. "Is he okay?"

"He is." He sounded so sure. "It happens less and less often these days, so each time it happens now, I tell myself that it might be the last time. And one of these times it will be."

"I certainly hope so. That poor man."

"He really is okay. His subconscious is still healing, but it *is* healing. Anyway, I hear you're starting a new job today."

"Yes, as weird as it is, I guess I'm going into the construction business."

He chuckled. "Not weird at all. My brother likes you and wants to help you."

Her cheeks got warm. Liked her? Like how a man liked a woman? She felt him staring at her and looked up.

"He wants you to stick around." Hudson was clearly uncomfortable. "I don't usually get involved in things like this, but if you're not interested in him, maybe you shouldn't take him up on his job offer."

She tried to follow what he was saying, but couldn't quite.

"Sorry, I didn't mean to suggest that there were strings attached." He visibly shuddered. "I just mean that if you're not interested, please make that clear to him so he won't have hope."

"Oh, I'm interested," she said quickly and then wished she hadn't. "Are you kidding? Of course I'm interested. Wyatt's amazing. But ..." Should she continue? He clearly wasn't enjoying this conversation, and Chase was going to be back any moment. "It's just hard for me to read him, so I'm glad you said that he liked me. Thank you for that."

"Hard to read him?" Now he sounded defensive of his brother. "Wyatt's an open book!"

He wasn't like any open book she'd ever seen. "I just mean he seems to change his mind a lot." She didn't want to call Wyatt moody, but despite her attempt at tact, Hudson's irritation grew.

"Wyatt might be the stubbornest person I know. I'm not sure I've ever heard him change his mind."

Now she almost looked forward to Chase returning. "I'm sorry. I didn't mean to speak ill of him. I just meant that I'm having trouble reading him. It's probably my fault, not his."

"I don't think it's anyone's fault. I just think it's hard to get to know someone. We want to put our best foot forward, but we also want them to know us. It's hard to balance what we share with what we don't share."

"I lost my mind and crashed into his barn. I think he's seen me at my worst."

"All the more reason to be completely honest with him." Something in his tone suggested that he believed she *wasn't* being completely honest with Wyatt. She scowled at Hudson.

"I am. I have been." She knew her words dripped with attitude, but she couldn't help it.

He nodded, clearly not believing her. "Good."

Chase came back inside, and Olivia went back to her cooking, trying to focus on the positive. Hudson had said that Wyatt liked her. That was huge. But this news was hard to reconcile with the man who had told his brothers "never ever." Maybe he hadn't liked her back then? That made sense. He'd probably thought she was crazy. So he'd *grown* to like her. That was great news. It suggested that he might grow to like her even more.

Chapter 24

Wyatt staggered into his kitchen and poured himself a cup of coffee, silently thanking God for the wonder of technology that was the coffee pot timer.

He hadn't slept much the night before. He couldn't stop thinking about Olivia. He was so crazy about her that he couldn't help planning out a future, but he had to keep checking himself. He shouldn't be thinking thoughts like that if it wasn't going to happen. He shouldn't be getting his hopes up. And if she couldn't even bring herself to tell him about the most significant thing in her life, probably the most significant thing that had ever happened to her, was there really any hope?

At one point in the middle of the night, he'd decided to come out with it, tell her that he knew—put all their cards on the table and then have an adult conversation. But since that big moment of strength in the dark quiet of his house, he'd talked himself out of it. If she didn't want him to know, then he didn't want to force that on her. Even though she wasn't acting it, she had to be stressed out, and he didn't want to add to her stress.

At least now she'll have health insurance, he told himself and took a long drink of his hot coffee.

He looked at the clock and groaned. He had to get moving. He contracted an HR firm to do all of his onboarding and management—he despised that paperwork stuff, and his company wasn't big enough to warrant his hiring an HR manager of his own.

Olivia needed to meet with that firm today and get all her paperwork filled out, but he knew that she wanted to be there when the insurance inspector showed up. He found his phone and texted her: Good morning. Do you know what time the insurance guy is coming?

She answered immediately: Between nine and three.

He chuckled as he wrote: Helpful that they're so specific. See you soon.

He glanced at the clock again even though he knew what it would say. It was way too early to call the HR people. He finished getting ready and then checked in with his other job sites before heading to the ranch. Finally, it was after nine, and he called his HR person, who promptly told him that no, she didn't make house calls. He explained that his new hire couldn't leave the ranch. "Then I guess she can't do any work today. Sorry."

He groaned, thanked her for her time, and hung up.

When he got to the ranch, Olivia was already working. He gently asked her to stop, not wanting a replay of the last time he'd caught her working without permission.

He explained the situation with HR. "So you can't officially do anything yet."

She frowned. She obviously thought that was silly, but she didn't know him as a professional. He was a rule follower.

"Let's do some planning instead." He looked around the extra-well-ventilated front barn. "And let's leave this as it is for now. We don't know yet what Hudson and Chase want to do with it." He waved her outside. "Come on. I'll show you what we're doing with the new barn."

She hurried to catch up to him.

"The framing is done. Next I want to add plumbing to the tack room and washroom."

"Plumbing?" Her alarm made him grin.

"Don't worry. It's all new plumbing, not the scary kind."

"I didn't know you were a plumber too."

"Oh yeah, I do the whole thing, from foundation to roof."

"Even electrical?"

"Even electrical." The admiration in her voice pleased him greatly.

"So how can I possibly help? I'm feeling so very unqualified right now."

"It's okay. I've hired lots of unqualified people before." He chuckled. "And most of them turned out great. I'll explain my plan and then show you how to put up the tack room walls. Then tomorrow you can probably get quite a bit of that done without me."

They stepped into the new barn, and the smell of new wood and hay washed over him. He loved those smells. He led her to the tack room and showed her the bare studs.

"Oh, I see," she said.

"There's still quite a bit of work to do. Originally, I was thinking this would be an ordinary tack room, but now I'm thinking of making it a bit more comfortable, maybe even adding a bathroom. That way, if your idea takes off, Chase will have an extra spot to hide out if he needs to."

Her eyes widened. "Do you really think my idea is going to take off?"

He nodded. "I'm not willing to bet the farm yet, but I saw it in Hudson's eyes. He wants it to happen. He loves being a doctor, but no one loves working sixty-hour weeks."

"Sixty hours?" she cried.

"That might be a small exaggeration, but yeah, he works a lot."

"I think running a wedding venue will be a lot of work too."

"Maybe. But he'll have all of us around to help him with that job." He flinched, wondering if he should have included her in the *us*, but he studied her carefully, and she didn't seem to mind.

Chapter 25

The insurance guy showed up at twenty minutes past three.

"You don't have to be here," he said after Olivia had introduced herself.

"Does that mean you want me to leave?"

He didn't answer her, and she started to feel really uncomfortable. She wished Wyatt were there. "I thought maybe you had some questions about what happened."

"*Should* I have questions?"

She didn't know. Wasn't that part of his job, to ask questions?

"Where's the truck?"

"In the shop."

"What shop? We didn't send a tow truck. Did you drive it to this *shop*?" The word *shop* dripped with irony as if he believed it didn't exist.

"I don't know why you guys couldn't find a tow truck driver. We managed to find one right away without so much as a

Google search." She knew she shouldn't be sassing this man, but she couldn't help it. "And *he towed* the *undriveable* truck to his *shop*. I don't know where it is. Somewhere close by."

"How am I supposed to evaluate it?"

"Was I supposed to leave it parked in the barn wall for four days? No one ever told me I couldn't have it towed, but I'm pretty sure it can be evaluated at the shop."

His disgust was obvious. "I'll need the name of the shop."

"I'll get it." She took her phone out of her pocket and texted Wyatt. She really wished he were here for this. She understood he had a company to run, but still, she really wished he were here.

"And you're staying here?" He looked at the house suspiciously.

"Just till the truck's fixed." No need to mention that she was now an employee of one of the Honeywood brothers.

"And how long have you known the residents?"

She really didn't like the way he was looking at her. Like she was a stupid idiot. That's the way Brian had looked at her. "I met them shortly after I accidentally drove my truck into their barn."

"And yet they're letting you stay with them?"

"Yes. Sir, this is South Dakota. Have you not been here long?"

He grimaced.

"It's the friendliest state in the country. They take their hospitality pretty seriously. And like I said, they're just helping me out till I get my truck back. I haven't moved in or anything."

"And you were on your way home from your wedding?"

"My canceled wedding, and no, I was on my way to a friend's house in Pierre."

"And none of these friendly South Dakotans would give you a ride to Pierre?"

She felt herself getting rattled and tried to stay strong. "I thought it would be easier to wait for my truck and give myself a ride."

"Uh-huh. I'll need to see this ranch's income tax filings for the last three years. Can you have those scanned and emailed to me, or should I ask your hosts directly?" Wow, his contempt ran deep.

He was waiting for her answer.

"If that's necessary, I will ask them to do that."

"I just told you it was necessary."

"And I'm going to verify that." She flashed him a plastic smile. "Verification can't hurt, right?"

"You know what I see? I see a failing horse ranch, an old worthless barn, and an unemployed scorned woman with an old pickup. It's the world's oldest con."

She highly doubted that. Surely people were conning one another long before there were insurance companies. "It's not a con. It was an accident."

He nodded. "Get me those tax returns. And I'll submit my report. You should hear from the company in thirty working days or less." He headed for his truck. She hadn't seen him take a single photograph.

She watched him drive away, feeling completely sunk. If they denied her claim, she was never going to be able to pay to get this barn fixed. When he was almost out of sight, she turned and trudged back to the house.

Chase stood in the kitchen window watching. When she stepped inside, he looked at her. "That didn't go well."

Was that a question or an observation? "No, it didn't."

"Hey, don't sweat it. It's only money."

That was easy for him to say. He wasn't the one in the hole.

"Really. We'd talked about tearing that barn down. It's not the end of the world if that has to happen."

She decided not to remind him that his brothers wanted to turn it into an event hall. She wasn't sure just how deep his denial ran. "Thank you for being so gracious."

He chuckled, and his eyes actually lit up a little. "I don't get called gracious very often. But really, Liv, it's no big deal."

She'd always hated it when people called her Liv, but coming from Chase, it felt kind of special.

Chapter 26

Usually, when Olivia was anywhere near a stove, she looked like she was dancing to her favorite song. This was not the case when Wyatt walked into his brothers' house on Wednesday evening. He stepped closer to her. "Hey, what's wrong?"

She sneaked a furtive glance in Chase's direction.

Wyatt looked at the pot on the stove. "Can that wait a minute?"

She shook her head. "I need to stir."

He reached over her hands, turned the burner off, and slid the pot away from her.

"Hey!" she cried, obviously insulted that he'd touched her pan.

"Let's, quite literally, put this on the back burner. Just for a minute."

She scowled at him.

"Come on. Just a quick walk." He walked away, hoping she'd follow and then held the door open for her when she did.

"I'm okay, really." She sniffed, avoiding his eyes.

"What happened?" Had Chase said something to upset her?

She took a deep breath and put her hands on her hips. "So I'm kind of freaking out a little because the insurance guy came and he was a total jerk, and he basically accused me of fraud and said I drove into your barn on purpose because your barn wasn't worth anything and my truck wasn't worth anything and so we cooked up this whole plan." She laughed hollowly. "And all this time my only comfort was that I was going to be able to give you a big wad of cash to make up for all the trouble, and now I'm afraid I'm not even going to be able to do that, and I just feel so bad, and you're going to have a big hole in your barn …" Her voice trailed off as the sobs took over. Wyatt had no choice but to take her into his arms, and though he expected it to feel good, he was startled by how right it felt. She fit there perfectly, melding into him like she was supposed to have been there all along.

"I'm sorry," she said, her voice muffled in his shoulder. "I'm just extra emotional because of …"

He knew why she was extra emotional. Hormones could really mess with a woman whose life was going exactly according to plan—he couldn't imagine what havoc hormones could wreak on top of Olivia's current situation. He rubbed her back and held her a little tighter.

They stood like this for a blissful minute. He was sorry that she was so upset, but he was glad for the excuse to hold her.

When her breathing calmed a little, he said, "It's okay. It's only money."

She laughed, and her body shook in his arms. "That's what Chase said too. What's with you Honeywoods?"

He shrugged. "Our mama raised us right."

She laughed again and leaned her head back to look at him. "Yes, yes, she did."

As if his lips had a mind of their own, they were on hers in a second. He kissed her tentatively at first, but when she returned the favor, his fingers found the back of her head, and her hair was every bit as soft as he'd known it would be.

It was the best kiss of his life, and he didn't want it to end—but then he remembered the baby, and he pulled away abruptly. She was obviously startled, and he felt bad, so he reached up and tenderly wiped away the remaining tears from her cheeks. He wanted to keep kissing her. He wanted to be her man, but she was emotionally frazzled from all the pregnancy hormones, and he didn't want to take advantage of that.

And why hadn't she told him about the baby yet? Why was she so intent on keeping that secret?

"I really like you, Olivia."

She blushed and looked down.

He gently tilted her chin up, and her eyes lifted to meet his again. "I like you too."

"I think we should be friends."

She giggled. "Uh, I think we're already friends."

He smiled, suddenly feeling more charming than usual. She made him feel good about himself. She made him feel like he could do anything.

"So as your friend, I want you to know that you can tell me anything. I won't judge you, and I want to help you."

Her brows drew together a little. "Okay." She stiffened in his arms.

He relaxed his grip a little.

"Do you think I'm holding some deep, dark secret?"

Well, no, he didn't think it was *dark*. "No, not at all. I just wanted you to know that you can trust me. With anything. I want to be there for you."

She nodded. "You are. You have been. And I'm grateful."

A chilly awkwardness wedged its way between them.

"I should probably get back to cooking."

He let go of her. "Yeah, okay. So tomorrow morning, you okay with going to see my HR person?"

She didn't look excited.

"I just want to make sure you have health insurance right away."

Suspicion clouded her eyes. "I'm not sick, Wyatt."

"I know," he said quickly.

"Or injured."

"I know that too."

"Okay." She walked toward the house, leaving him standing there like a fool. She didn't look back at him, and she held her chin up high.

His stomach rumbled, and he followed her inside. She ignored him as she went back to work, and he went into the living room, surprised to see Dustin in there. "Hey, where did you come from?"

Dustin laughed. "Same place you did. Mom and Dad."

Wyatt rolled his eyes. "I didn't see your truck."

"I parked over by the new barn. I had to unload some stuff I got for Chase at the auction."

"Oh." Wyatt sat down.

"And now I'm lingering because I keep hearing all about this new cook you hired."

"I didn't hire her as a cook."

"Right. Then what did you hire her for?"

"As a laborer."

Dustin gave him a patronizing look. "Sure. Why'd you really hire her?"

"No, really. She's a laborer. She can do it. I promise."

"I don't doubt it, but why'd you hire her? You haven't been looking for help for over a year."

Wyatt looked over his shoulder to make sure she wasn't sneaking up on them. Then he lowered his voice. "I like her, and she needs health insurance—"

"Why, is she sick?" he asked too loudly.

"No, no. She just feels better having it. More secure, I guess. Anyway, she wanted to work at the jail, and I was worried that wasn't safe, so I panicked and offered her a job."

Dustin stared at him, still being condescending. "Wouldn't it have been easier just to marry her?"

He'd probably meant it as a joke, but it hit Wyatt as an epiphany. How had he not thought of that? Sure, it was too soon to be thinking about marriage. He'd only just met her. But marrying her would certainly make it simple to insure her. And since she was pregnant, maybe he *should* be thinking about marrying her. It was too soon, sure, but wasn't a baby a good reason to speed up the timeline?

"Does she have a sister?" Dustin asked.

"She does not."

"That's a bummer."

Chapter 27

Again, Olivia did not sleep well. This time she couldn't stop thinking about that kiss. That kiss that could've melted rocks.

She couldn't believe she'd almost admitted that she was crying because that stupid insurance bully had reminded her of Brian. She was so glad she'd been able to stop herself. But then he'd asked her to share her secrets, like he'd known she was holding something back. How had he known?

Maybe because you didn't finish your sentence, you big oaf. I'm just really emotional because ... She had practically begged him to fill in the blanks himself. Whoops. She hadn't meant to do that. But she surely wasn't going to admit to Mr. Wonderful that she was still crying over her stupid ex.

Her phone rang at a few minutes till eight. It was Rodney, telling her that her truck was fixed. She was grateful, but she was also a little worried that now she had to pay the bill. She asked him if the inspector had been there to look at it. No, he hadn't, but he had called with some questions. "Not exactly a pleasant fella," Rodney said.

"No, no. He sure isn't. Thank you. I'll get a ride into town as soon as I can so I can get my old girl out of your hair."

"No worries. You can always call an Uber." She didn't know if he was kidding, but then she heard him cackling as he hung up.

What a funny guy.

Hudson was already gone for the day, and Wyatt hadn't arrived yet. Her only choice was Chase. She approached him tentatively.

When she got close, he looked at her warily.

"Going to be a nice day out," she said lamely.

"It already is. What can I do for you?"

"Feel free to say no, but Rodney just called, and my truck is ready, and I was wondering if you would mind giving me a lift into town." She braced herself for the rejection, but he didn't give one. The silence made her uncomfortable, so she added, "He said I could call myself an Uber, but I think he was joking."

Chase laughed quietly. "In West Hope? Yeah, I think he was joking. Although I hear they exist in Rapid City, so you could probably get one. You'd just be waiting a while."

She didn't know what to say. He wasn't answering her question. She was about to give up and walk away when he said, "Give me one second. I'll meet you at the truck."

One second? She needed more than a second! She ran inside, panicked for a full thirty seconds before locating her wallet, and then ran back outside. Sure enough, Chase was behind the wheel. She scrambled up into the truck. "Thanks so much for this."

He grunted.

And that grunt was the last thing he said before pulling into the small lot in front of Goober Pyle Garage.

She thanked him again, expecting another grunt, but she didn't get one. She quickly slid out of the cab, grateful to shut the door on the most awkward lift of her life. He drove away, and she turned to look at the garage. Was this the right place?

Then she saw her old truck parked out back. Yep, this was the right spot. She headed for the door.

A bell jingled over her head when she entered, and a man in blue coveralls soon appeared. An embroidered tag told her this was Rodney, or at least that it was someone wearing Rodney's coveralls.

"Hi. I'm Olivia. The owner of the blue Chevy."

He flashed a genial smile. "Hi Olivia. I'm Rodney. Do you want to go take a look at the old girl, make sure she's up to snuff?"

"I think it will be okay?" She wasn't sure she'd be able to discern anything by looking at it. As long as the engine ran, and the wheels spun, she would be happy.

"Like I said, the frame was okay. I banged out some dents, but you can definitely tell there was some damage. And I replaced the grill. I found an old bumper off the same model, so that didn't cost you much. The expensive part was the repairs to your steering system." He seemed to realize she wasn't quite following. "If Wyatt has any questions, tell him to give me a ring." He smiled again and handed her a slip.

The total due was painful, but it wasn't as bad as she'd feared it might be, so she was grateful. "Probably should have asked you before you started working ..." She laughed awkwardly. "But do you take plastic?"

"Oh, of course. With a lead in like that, I thought you were going to ask me if I take traveler's checks."

"What's a traveler's check?"

"I'm not really sure either, but I had a woman ask me if I would take them once. I politely said no thank you." He laughed and took the credit card out of her hand.

Chapter 28

Seth Honeywood was feeling left out. Everyone was talking about Wyatt's new flame, and he wanted to get the scoop directly from the source. So he figured out which job site Wyatt was working on, and he showed up there at lunchtime.

Wyatt headed his way as soon as he saw him.

Seth jumped out of the truck and dropped his tailgate.

"Hey, Wyatt. How are things with your new sweetheart?"

Wyatt chuckled dryly. "I wouldn't say she's my sweetheart yet."

"What are you waiting for? Dustin says he cracked a joke about marrying her, and that you looked near ready to propose."

"Come on over for supper tonight," he said, avoiding the unasked question.

"Okay, I will. But you better be careful. If she can cook as good as everybody's saying, I might just steal her for myself."

"Don't you dare."

"But for real, you know she got her truck back today, right?"

"I didn't know that, but I knew it was going to happen soon. Rodney does quick work."

"Well, you know what that means."

"No, what?" Wyatt took a bite of his sandwich.

"It means she's free to fly the coop! You need to ask her out on a proper date before she gives up on you and drives off into the sunset."

"Since when are you a love expert?"

That smarted a little, and Seth considered dropping the whole thing. Fine then, he wouldn't help. "I'm not claiming to be an expert." Far from it, actually. "But I know that women like to go out on dates. Doesn't take an expert to know that."

"We've spent lots of time together."

"Yeah, *with your brothers.* Come on, man, what is the problem? Did Dustin get it wrong? Are you not actually into her?"

"No, I like her." He sighed.

Something was weighing on his brother. "What is it?"

"It's complicated."

"What? Is it the other guy? I heard he was a real jerk."

"He is, and sort of."

"Oh will you please just tell me? I can't help if you don't tell me."

He sighed again. "I could use some advice, but I really need you to not tell anyone."

"Who am I gonna tell?"

"Hudson, Chase, Dustin, Burke."

"What?" Seth cried. "None of them know either?"

"I don't know for sure that Hudson doesn't know, but no, I don't think he does."

Wyatt had lost his mind. He was speaking in riddles. "You better spit it out, or I'm going to try to thump it out of you."

Wyatt laughed. "Okay, but it stays between us?"

"Whatever."

"Never mind then."

"Fine, fine. It stays between us." Good grief, this had better be one juicy secret to be worthy of all this drama.

"She's pregnant, and she won't tell me."

Seth felt his jaw fall open, and it took effort to close it again. "Come again?"

"You heard me."

"What do you mean she won't tell you? Then how do you know?"

"That first night, it was raining, and her dress was soaking wet. It was glued to her body. I could just tell. I could see it."

"Are you sure? Maybe she just had too many twinkies."

Wyatt gave him a dirty look. "I'm sure. She's not overweight. She had a little bit of a baby bump. That's all."

Seth exhaled slowly with a whistle. "Wow man, that's pretty heavy. So she doesn't know that you know?"

"Correct. And for some reason, she won't tell me."

"Well, duh! She probably thinks you'll run for the hills if you find out."

"I wouldn't do that."

"Probably not, but think about it, man. Think about all the men you know. Most of them would take off running in the other direction. And she just met you. And she's coming off a horrible relationship. So she might well be assuming that you are just like the other guys she's known."

Wyatt looked a little pale.

"The man she left at the altar, he's the father?"

"Don't say it like that. She didn't leave him at the altar. His girlfriend showed up and broke up their wedding. It wasn't Olivia's fault."

"Okay." Seth didn't really care about that part of the story. "But is that dude the father?"

Wyatt hesitated. "If she won't tell me that she's pregnant, she certainly hasn't told me who the father is. But I would assume so, yes."

"So if you pursue this, you're tangling yourself up with that guy for the next eighteen years. Actually more than that."

"Huh?"

Poor Wyatt. He hadn't thought this through. "So you have to deal with this guy while you're making your step-kid's schedule. You have to see him and his new lady at all the baseball games, assuming he'll care enough to go, and if he doesn't care, then you can deal with your step-kid being all depressed about that. Either way, he'll probably be at the graduation and the wedding and the—"

"I think you've made your point."

"Sorry, man," Seth said. "I'm not saying it won't be worth it, but you're right, this is complicated."

Wyatt didn't say anything.

"Eat your lunch." Seth crunched on a chip, thinking. Wyatt was a good man. He deserved a good woman. Seth wasn't sure this was the right move for Wyatt. But there was such a thing as giving too much advice.

"I don't want to do the wrong thing. If the three of them are supposed to be a family, who am I to interfere with that?"

"That's a good question."

"Yeah, and honestly, it's one I wished I'd never thought of."

"But if he's not interested in being a real man and taking care of his family then you get to swoop in and be a hero."

Wyatt took a swig of his coke. "I wouldn't use the word *hero*, but yeah. That would be grand." He took another bite of his sandwich.

"So I guess you need to know what his intentions are."

"How am I supposed to know that?"

Seth shrugged. "Only one way I can think of to find out."

Wyatt groaned. "I really don't want to talk to that guy again."

"Again?"

Wyatt told him about the time a stubby toad had tried to chase him off mommy-toad's lawn.

Seth couldn't help but laugh. "Wow, I've missed a lot. Sorry. I need to hang around the ranch more, I guess."

"I've been hanging around there a lot lately. Chase might want a break from all the company."

"Nah, Chase doesn't count me as company. Anyway, so you going to go see him?"

"Chase?"

"You know what I mean. The toad."

"I don't know." Wyatt balled up his sandwich wrapper and slid off the tailgate. "Maybe I have to."

Chapter 29

Wyatt had no idea how to find Brian, so he drove to his mother's house. Connie answered the door looking like any other kind, innocent South Dakotan woman. Too bad Wyatt knew different. "Good evening, ma'am. I'm Wyatt Honeywood." The name obviously didn't ring a bell. "And I'm looking for Brian."

"Brian?" Now she looked suspicious. "How do you know Brian?"

He thought it best not to get into it.

Her eyes darkened. "Oh. You're the one who came with Olivia."

"Yes, ma'am. And I really need to talk to Brian. It's important." Did this woman know about the baby? He wanted to believe that she didn't. If she did, then surely she would have behaved differently with Olivia's belongings, right?

"I don't know where he is." She started to shut the door.

He stopped it with his hand. "Please. I'm trying to do a good thing here. I mean him no ill will." This was only a small lie. He should have said that he promised not to act on all the ill will that he felt toward him.

Her face twisted into a sour expression. "Go to the Dairy Queen. I'll call him. If he wants to meet you, he'll show up. If he doesn't, he won't. Either way, don't come back here."

"Why are you so angry with Olivia?" Wyatt couldn't help asking. This woman had everything so backward.

"Are you kidding? She broke my baby's heart." She slammed the door.

Wyatt went back to his truck, trying to remember where the Spearfish Dairy Queen was. He found it soon enough and then sat there waiting. He was just about to give up and get a Dilly Bar for the ride home, when a lifted truck pulled into the lot. He didn't know what Brian drove, and he couldn't see this driver's face, and yet he knew. That was exactly the truck a stubby toad would drive. The windows were even tinted. How had Olivia fallen for this?

He pulled into the parking spot beside Wyatt and rolled down his window. He didn't turn his engine off, which was louder than it should have been. "What?" he said from his position a foot above Wyatt.

"We need to talk about the baby."

The color drained from the toad's face. "What? What baby?"

Was this guy playing stupid? "Are you telling me that you don't know that Olivia is pregnant?"

"Well, if she is, I had nothing to do with it!"

What? Wyatt stared at him stupidly.

"Olivia isn't that kind of girl. Why do you think I had to go elsewhere for affection?"

Something in Wyatt's stomach curdled. Olivia had dated him for years, and they'd never slept together? He had a whole newfound respect for her.

"If she's pregnant, it's not mine." He threw the truck into reverse. "Stay out of Spearfish," he said as if he owned the whole town.

Wyatt watched him drive away, his mind swimming in a sea of confusing doubts. He knew what he'd seen. That had been a baby bump. But he wasn't going on that memory alone. It was also her obsession with health insurance. And she'd practically admitted that she was hormonal.

She was pregnant. She had to be. But if Brian wasn't the father, who was? Did Wyatt have this all wrong? Was Olivia the best con artist ever? If she was the one who cheated on Brian, that explained so much. It explained why none of her friends would help her, why his mother had thrown her belongings out into the rain, and why she hated him so much.

He felt ill.

He'd been wrong.

He'd been conned.

It was the only way all these facts added up.

He started the truck and pointed it toward West Hope. *Don't jump to conclusions*, a voice in his head argued. *You know Olivia. She's not a liar.* Except that he didn't know her. Not really. He'd only known her for a few days, and he could easily have been blinded by her beauty. Maybe he'd been so busy trying to make her into the woman he wanted her to be that he'd totally missed who she really was.

He wasn't going to figure this out unless he talked to Olivia. And no more patience. It was time for honest, open communication, whether she was ready or not.

Chapter 30

Something was wrong with Wyatt. He'd gotten to the ranch halfway through supper and wouldn't even look her in the eye.

Something was wrong with his brother Seth too, who had shown up uninvited to eat with them. This was okay with her of course. It wasn't her ranch. But she found it strange that he'd just popped up out of nowhere, and her unease was made stronger by the fact that he kept looking at her stomach. Halfway through the meal, she excused herself to go put on a sweatshirt. Everyone complimented her cooking, everyone but Wyatt. When she was clearing the dishes, he walked out the front door.

Seriously? He was going to leave without even saying anything? The day after he told her that he liked her? She didn't care what Hudson said. Wyatt was the moodiest man on earth. She chased him outside. "What is wrong with you?"

He whirled around. "What? Nothing is wrong with me!" He put his hands on his hips. "I came intent on talking to you, but I decided

I should probably wait till tomorrow. I'm really tired." He didn't sound tired.

She took a step closer. She didn't want to spend the whole night wondering what she'd done wrong. "Just spit it out, Wyatt. What's wrong?"

He stared at her.

"Spit it out!" she screeched.

"Fine! Did you cheat on Brian?"

His words sucked the air out of her lungs. She must have heard him wrong. "What did you just say to me?"

He didn't repeat himself.

"You've lost your mind."

"Maybe. But you haven't answered the question."

"I don't need to answer your question. I don't answer to you. In fact, I'm not giving you another single ounce of my energy or another second of my time. I quit this fake job you cooked up for me, and I quit you, Wyatt Honeywood. You never have to see me again. Have a nice life." She turned to go inside, focusing on not crying. *Just stay angry*, she told herself. *You can cry later when you're far, far away from here.*

Hudson, Chase, and weird Seth all stared at her when she came inside. "Sorry, Hudson, I can't do the dishes tonight."

"Oh that's all right," he said, his concern obvious.

She didn't know how much they might have heard, but she knew that Wyatt and she had been pretty loud.

Chase didn't look at her, but there was sympathy written on his face, and he went straight to the sink, pushing his sleeves up on the way.

She hurried into her room, threw all of her stuff into bags and boxes, and then headed for the door, angry that she wasn't going to be able to get it all in one trip.

"Do you want some help?" Hudson asked.

"No, thank you. I've got it." She didn't want any more help from the Honeywood brothers. She'd already accepted too much of their charity.

When she opened the front door with her foot, she realized part of her had been hoping that Wyatt would be there, hat in hand, maybe a rose in his teeth, ready to fall on his knees and apologize, but he wasn't there.

And that was a good thing. Because he was a crazy person. A crazy, mean person. Cheat on Brian? Where had that come from? He must have been *trying* to hurt her, which made him a crazy, sadistic jerk.

She tossed her things into the cab of her truck and then hurried back inside the house for the rest of her stuff.

Hudson was on the phone when she got back inside. She assumed that he was calling Wyatt and became incensed. She needed to get away from both Wyatt and Hudson. What a strange twist of fate that Chase had become her favorite Honeywood.

She took a deep breath and then tried to keep her voice steady. "Hudson and Chase, thank you for your hospitality. I will send you a check for the barn the second that I have the funds." Hudson started to say something, probably going to tell her not to worry about it, but she didn't give him the time. She was back out the door in seconds.

By the time she got behind the wheel, her whole body was shaking, and she had no idea where she was going.

Maybe she needed to get away from West Hope. Pick a different small town with an equally encouraging name and start over there instead.

Yeah, maybe she'd do just that, but not tonight. She had learned her lesson about driving upset. So she focused on keeping it between the lines and headed to the closest lodging, a small chain motel on the edge of town.

There were plenty of rooms available, and she took the first one they offered. Then she hurried inside, slid the deadbolt into place, and promptly burst into tears.

She undressed, crawled between the sheets still crying, silently thanked God that they were so clean, and then cried herself to sleep.

Chapter 31

Seth showed up for a job site lunch again on Friday.

"This is getting to be a regular thing." Wyatt wasn't sure this was a tradition he wanted to create. He'd followed Seth's advice last time, and look what had happened. Wyatt was weak with confusion and sick with guilt.

Seth grabbed his cooler out of the back seat. "How are you holding up?"

Wyatt lowered Seth's tailgate himself, eager to sit. "Right now I'm just tired," he lied.

"Late night?"

He opened his pop can. "I haven't been sleeping well lately." This was an entirely new problem for him. Before Olivia, he'd never encountered insomnia.

"Gotta get you some of Hudson's herbal tea. So what happened in Spearfish? I was going to ask you last night, but you didn't really seem in the mood."

Wyatt groaned. "Don't need to talk about it."

"I wish you would. I'm worried that I gave you terrible advice."

Wyatt thought that maybe he had, but making Seth feel guilty wasn't going to help anything. "I don't know what to think. That toad said it couldn't possibly be his baby. That's what happened in Spearfish."

"Really?"

Wyatt didn't say anything else. He tried to enjoy his coke.

"Wyatt, that doesn't seem right. I don't even know her, and I know she's not the type."

"Not the type to what?"

"She's not the type to cheat on her fiancé and then lie about it to you. Man, are you *sure* she's pregnant?"

Yes, he was sure, but he stayed quiet. He was tired of talking.

"Seriously, man. I believe that you saw what you saw, but that's the simplest explanation to this rat's nest. Think about it, and really try to be objective. She hasn't told you that she's pregnant. He said she couldn't possibly be pregnant. Man, I really stared at her stomach the other night. I'm no expert, but I don't think she's pregnant."

He sighed. "I've spent a lot of time with her. I'm not an idiot. She's pregnant. But it doesn't matter. She hates me."

"She doesn't hate you. She's falling in love with you."

"Who told you that?"

"Hudson."

Wyatt rolled his eyes. His brothers were turning into a bunch of high school cheerleaders. "Well, that was yesterday. I'm pretty sure she hates me now." At least he would hate him if he were her.

"Well you've only got two choices. It's pretty simple."

"What might those be?" he asked dryly.

"You either explain yourself and apologize, or you give up and walk away."

He didn't know which of those would hurt worse. One would hurt his pride. The other would break his heart.

"You've got some time to think about it, but don't wait too long."

He really hated taking advice from his little brother. He hated that he needed the advice. Most of all, he hated that his little brother was right. *How have I made such a mess of things?* "Let's talk about something else."

"Sure. We don't have to talk at all." He pushed his party-sized bag of chips across the tailgate. "Here, have some chips. They do a body good."

Wyatt ate his fill of chips and then spent the rest of the day agonizing over his two choices. And by the end of the day he'd decided that there was only one thing that really mattered here, and it wasn't his pride. It wasn't even his level of heartbreak.

The only thing that he should be considering was Olivia's heart. She'd been stomped on by Brian. Then Wyatt had kicked her when she was down. None of this was her fault.

And he had to make it right. But first he had to find her. Hudson had told him that she'd left the ranch, and no one had heard from her since.

He released his guys a few minutes early, forced a smile when he told them to have a good weekend, and then texted her, asking if they could meet somewhere for a short chat. When she didn't answer him right away, he didn't panic, but as the minutes and then the hours ticked by, he started to worry that she wasn't going to answer him at all.

At eight o'clock, he texted, "I need to apologize. I don't want to let another whole night go by without telling you how much I care about you. Please give me a chance, and then if you want to, I'll let you walk away without bothering you again. Can we please meet somewhere? It will only take a few minutes."

His hopeful heart didn't give up until after midnight. Then he started trying to come to terms with the idea that she wasn't going to give him that chance.

Olivia Long was done with him, and he couldn't blame her.

Chapter 32

Olivia was so excited to go to the library. She was furious with herself that she'd lost the jail job—thrown it away, in fact. And for what? The vain hope that she was going to find love with some gorgeous cowboy? What had she been thinking? There was a reason he was still single: Wyatt Honeywood was insane.

It had taken every ounce of her self-control not to answer his texts, and she was a little proud of herself for managing. The man had a way with words, so she was glad she'd gotten out when she did. She didn't need to spend the rest of her life riding the hot and cold wave of a silver-tongued shapeshifter. She'd be insane before she hit their tenth anniversary.

She got to the library early, and the librarian didn't exactly seem happy to see her. "I wasn't sure you would show up since you ghosted my sister."

Olivia suppressed a groan. "I didn't mean to do that, and I regret it very much."

The woman's expression softened. "Did you do it for love or money?"

"Love," she answered quickly.

She nodded in commiseration. "Most of us have made that mistake."

"And it really was a mistake. It wasn't even love. I just thought it could be."

"Well, better you find out now than later. I always wondered why those Honeywood brothers were all still single."

Good grief, did the whole town know her business? She knew the woman was trying to be supportive, but her words made Olivia feel defensive of Hudson and Chase. She kept it to herself, though. She didn't really know them, and if she'd been so wrong about Wyatt, maybe she'd been wrong about them too.

Her library training took a little more than an hour. "You'll face the occasional more complicated issue, but this is my day off, and I want to get home. So if anyone asks you for something other than checking out a book, tell them they'll have to come back on Monday."

"You're not open tomorrow?"

"We are, but someone else works tomorrow."

That was too bad. Olivia would have gobbled up those hours if they were available. She grew nervous when her new boss left, but then a weird giddiness fell over her. She was all alone in this large, beautiful place. The silence was almost supernaturally comforting.

For more than forty minutes, no one patronized the library, and then a pretty woman came in, smiled at her, and plunked a stack of romance novels down on her counter.

"Thank you," Olivia said and then was happy to scan them into the system. This job was unexpectedly fun.

The woman returned a few minutes later with a stack of paperbacks. She smiled again as she handed Olivia her library card.

Olivia thanked her and scanned the card, and that's when she noticed the name: Ava Honeywood. She looked up, startled.

"What's wrong?"

"Oh sorry, nothing."

Ava squinted at her. "You're Olivia, aren't you?"

Oh boy. "Yeah. How'd you know?"

Ava's smile was sincere and comforting. "I heard about you, I heard you were looking for a job in town, and then you went pale at the sign of my name." She smiled. "I'm Burke's wife."

"Oh. Sorry! Someone told me that none of Wyatt's brothers were married."

Ava laughed lightly. "Yeah, sometimes people forget that Burke exists. He's sort of the black sheep, and he's not around much."

What did that mean? Her question must have shown on her face because Ava expounded. "He's usually chasing a rodeo."

"Oh. You don't go with him?"

She laughed again. "No, one of us has to work to pay the bills."

"Oh. Sorry."

"No, don't be. He's a good man." She sounded sincere, but she studied the countertop in front of her when she said it.

"Well, it's nice to meet you." Olivia slid the books closer to her. "Enjoy your books."

"Thanks." She acted like she was going to walk away, but then she stopped. "So, are you and Wyatt going to work out, you think?"

Ava obviously hadn't been privy to the most recent update.

"I don't think so."

She looked surprised. "No? Why not?"

Oh boy, where to begin? She tried to think of a way to politely summarize the situation. She couldn't badmouth Wyatt to his sister-in-law. "Nothing bad, really. He's just really moody, and I don't like roller coasters."

Ava's eyes widened in surprise. "Moody? Wyatt? Really?" She laughed uneasily. "He must behave differently when he's in love."

Olivia didn't know what to say to that.

"I've never seen that man have any mood at all. Of all the brothers, I would say he's the steadiest, the most stable."

Olivia had no desire to argue with the woman. "I guess I just brought it out of him." She forced a smile. "It's okay, really. Some things just aren't meant to be."

"Yeah. Maybe." It seemed she wanted to say more. "Well, if I can't welcome you to the family, I can at least welcome you to West Hope." She didn't say the town's name with the same affection that everyone else seemed to.

"Have you lived here long?"

"Oh yeah. Forever." She smiled and clutched her stack of paperbacks to her chest. "See you around, Olivia."

"You too. Nice to meet you."

Ava started toward the door but then stopped and turned back. "I'm sorry. I don't want to be nosy, but this story just isn't adding up. And I'm not saying you have to give me the missing info, but if you're the one who's missing the info, well, make sure you get all of it before you give up on him for good, okay? He's a good man. And he doesn't show interest in women very often. He's hard to impress. And well, you impressed him. That's not nothing." She smiled and then left the library for real.

Olivia was excited to go to church on Sunday morning—until she pulled her old truck into the crowded parking lot. Then nerves overcame her. She was a fairly confident woman, but it was still uncomfortable walking into a new place alone.

She took a deep breath, checked her makeup in the rearview, and then psyched herself up for a few seconds before getting out of the truck. Then she held her head high as she ordered her feet to stride across the parking lot.

It was muddy, and she was glad her only choice of footwear had been practical. She didn't normally wear tennis shoes to church, but today, it had been a good idea. The ground had that spring softness to it *before* they had gotten all the rain the night before. Now it was downright soupy.

But she made it across the lot and up the steps, where she shook a stranger's hand and then stepped into the building.

When Olivia had been looking online for a church in West Hope, she'd seen that there were a lot of them. So it had never occurred to her to worry that she might accidentally choose the same church that Wyatt attended.

But that's exactly what she'd done.

And it wasn't just Wyatt. There was a whole row of them.

She recognized him from the back before he'd had a chance to see her. She would know those shoulders anywhere, so broad, so strong—he started to turn around.

Yikes! She dove sideways and ducked at the same time, inadvertently ending up hiding in a crouch behind a woman in a wheelchair. This was terrible of course, and she immediately began looking for a way to undo what she'd just done. This brought her eye to eye and nearly nose to nose with a boy of about six, who stared at her with wide and slightly judgmental eyes. She wanted to explain, "He almost caught me staring at his shoulders," but she knew he wouldn't understand.

Instead, she gave him her best, I'm-an-adult-so-it's-okay-if-I-act-like-this smile and then turned and tried to duckwalk out of the sanctuary. This would have been unfortunate enough without the fact that it brought her eye level with the bottom of many skirts, which made the whole thing so much more suspicious.

"Did you lose a contact?"

She looked up to see Dustin Honeywood staring down at her.

Oh no. She was so busted. She shook her head, still in her crouch.

Dustin shocked her by crouching down in front of her, as if he were about to talk to a small child. She'd learned that Seth was the youngest brother, but Dustin acted like he was.

He tried to whisper something, but everyone was milling about them excitedly greeting one another, so it was too loud for whispering. He shook his head and started over, now sort of whisper-shouting. "I can help you get out of here, but he's already seen you, so you might want to just stand up."

She wanted to cry. "Has he seen me crouching?" she whisper-shouted back.

Dustin didn't say no, and his wince suggested that yes, Wyatt had seen her acting like an utter fool.

Again.

And just how was Dustin going to help her get out of there? Did he know of a secret underground tunnel?

He stood and then offered her a hand, which she accepted. He pulled her to her feet, and she slowly turned to face the music.

Literally.

The piano had started playing. Her eyes locked with Wyatt's, and she tried to keep her chin high as she slid into the back row. She could feel his eyes on her but refused to return his gaze, and then when she couldn't stand it anymore and did look up, he had turned back around. There they all were, all lined up in the fourth row. Five brothers. They were only missing Ava's husband. Olivia scanned the sanctuary but didn't see Ava either. She couldn't blame her. She wouldn't want to come without her husband either.

Olivia tried to focus on the music, which was really quite lovely, but she couldn't stop thinking about Wyatt. She was confused. She was still angry, but she missed him. *Good grief, girl, pick a lane!* She wanted to talk to him, wanted to smell that sawdust and laundry soap smell of him, wanted to feel his arms around her again. But she was also still furious. He'd accused her of cheating on Brian! How was she supposed to get over that?

When the music ended, and Wyatt turned to sit, he looked at her, and what she saw in his eyes made her heart shiver with sudden cold.

Wyatt was sad. Like *really* sad. Maybe even depressed.

Had she done that? No, of course not. And if she had, he totally deserved it. But if that were true, why was her anger slowly seeping out of her? She tried to focus on the sermon and then nearly cried out in agony when she realized the point of the message was forgiveness. Seven times seventy, Jesus said.

Okay, fine. She would let Wyatt apologize, and she would probably forgive him. She was quickly becoming aware that she really did want to give him one more chance.

But that was it. If he hurt her again, she had to move on. Because she wasn't going to be in an emotionally unhealthy relationship ever again.

Feeling good about her decision, she enjoyed the rest of the service. But when she picked her head up after the closing prayer, Wyatt was nowhere to be seen.

She thought about texting him but decided against it. If he had wanted to talk to her, he wouldn't have left the service early.

There was only one reason he would have done that: He didn't want to talk to her. He'd given her a chance to give him a chance, and she'd squandered it.

This was over before it had ever really begun.

Chapter 33

Doctor Hudson Honeywood enjoyed a group practice with one other doctor in downtown West Hope, but he still had to do the occasional shift at the hospital. He didn't look forward to these shifts because they were quite stressful, but he had to admit: they were also interesting.

Monday morning found him filling one of these shifts in the emergency room. He pulled the cubicle curtain shut behind him and smiled at the senior man sitting on the exam table. "Good morning, Mr. Cotton. You're having stomach pains?"

"Not yet."

Hudson did a double take. "Then where is your pain?" He dragged a stool over with his foot and sat down.

"I don't have any yet." Mr. Cotton was sounding impatient.

Hudson set his clipboard on his lap. "How can I help you today, sir?"

"My wife poisoned me."

"Do you know what she gave you?"

He shook his head slowly, dramatically. "It was in my eggs. I thought they tasted funny, but she said, 'Oh no, it's just your eggs the same way I've made them for fifty years.'"

"But it wasn't the same?"

"No, she told me afterward that she'd poisoned them."

"Okay." Hudson was a bit flummoxed. "I can give you some charcoal, but we really need to know what she gave you so we can respond accordingly. Can you ask her?"

He shook his head. "She won't tell me."

Hudson wasn't entirely convinced that the man had been poisoned, but he couldn't exactly ignore the complaint. "Mr. Cotton, I'm going to involve the police, so I just want to make sure. Are you sure that she poisoned you?"

He shrugged. "She says she did."

"And what's your wife's name?"

"Beverly."

"Okay. Excuse me for one second." He stepped out of the cubicle and called the Sheriff's Department. He gave them Mr. Cotton's name, his wife's name, and their street address."

"Oh ..." the deputy said. "*That* Mr. Cotton."

"What is it?"

"Beverly Cotton died a year ago. We responded to a call there last week when he said she'd run off. He was panicking because he couldn't find her."

Hudson's heart sank. "Okay. You're sure?"

"Unless there's another Doug and Beverly Cotton living on North Bugle Street, then, yeah, I'm sure."

Hudson hung up and returned to the cubicle. "Mr. Cotton, did you drive yourself here?"

"I did. Figured I could get here before the poison kicked in."

"Okay. The good news is, you're going to be okay. We are going to give you something for your stomach, and you'll soon be fit as a fiddle. But that medication might make you a bit drowsy, so do you have a loved one I could call? Someone who could come get you?"

"My granddaughter is a nurse. She might be able to come get me."

"Great. What's her name?" He wrote it down. "Do you know her phone number?"

"I don't have it on me. Beverly knows it by heart."

Oh dear. "Do you know where your granddaughter works?"

"Sure. Of course I do. She works at the cancer care center." His obvious pride at this warmed Hudson's heart.

"She must be a very good nurse."

"She is. You should hire her here."

Hudson smiled. "I'm going to go try to track her down. You sit tight and relax." He stepped out again, pausing on his way to the phone to tell a nurse to give Mr. Cotton a liquid antacid. "If he asks any questions, tell him I'll answer them when I get back." He called the cancer center and after a few minutes, got Evelyn Cotton on the line.

Her voice was lovely. He briefly explained the situation, and she interrupted to say, "Oh, Nana. She used to joke all the time about how she'd poisoned his breakfast. Poor Grampa. He must be so confused. I'll be right there."

Hudson thanked her, hung up, and returned to the cubicle to update Mr. Cotton—who was snoring. Hudson closed the curtain to let him rest and then went to greet his next patient.

A screaming toddler was pulling on his earlobe, and understandably, the young mom was panicking. The nurse was ushering them both into an exam room when Hudson's peripheral vision caught sight of someone familiar.

He stepped away for just a second to make sure he'd seen what he thought he'd seen.

He had.

He returned to the counter. "I need to get this kid out of pain, but can you call my brother Wyatt?" He couldn't go chasing after a gurney, no matter who he'd seen on it. He needed to help this boy, and he didn't want to stray too far from Mr. Cotton.

The nurse nodded, her brow furrowed in confusion. "What do you want me to say?"

"Tell him that everyone's fine." Hudson didn't know this to be true, but he was hoping. "And tell him to get down here. I need to talk to him."

"Sure thing, Doctor."

Hudson left her and joined the mother and child behind the curtain. But before he threw all of his energy and attention at this child, he silently said a prayer for Olivia.

Chapter 34

Wyatt asked the nurse three times before accepting that she didn't know why he was being summoned to the hospital. The only theory he could come up with was that something was wrong with Hudson, but if that were the case, wouldn't that nurse know about it?

He hadn't heard any panic in her voice, which was his only comfort as he sped from his job site to the hospital.

When he got there, he called Hudson and wasn't surprised when Hudson didn't pick up. He was either busy helping someone in a health crisis or he was having a health crisis himself. Either way, he probably wasn't sitting around staring at his phone.

Wyatt went to the front desk. Since he didn't know what he was doing there, he didn't know how to tell them why he was there. "I got a message from my brother Dr. Honeywood to come down here. I don't know why." He tried to keep the panic out of his voice.

He knew this woman was a volunteer and that she had to deal with frantic people all the time.

She did look confused, and she made a phone call before telling him that Hudson would meet him in the emergency room waiting room.

Wyatt's stomach churned. Maybe it was one of his brothers. Was it Burke? He tried to remember where Burke was right now, and he couldn't, but he was pretty sure that he wasn't in West Hope, and if he'd been hurt at a rodeo somewhere, he wouldn't be in the West Hope emergency room. *Just breathe*, he told himself. No need to panic over a crisis that didn't exist yet. He was shaving years off his life with all this fear.

True to his word, Hudson was waiting in the ER.

"What is it?"

"She's okay."

"Who? Ava?" Ava was the only *she* in their family.

"No. Olivia."

Wyatt's knees went weak, and he sank into the nearest chair. "What's wrong with Olivia?"

"Appendicitis. I didn't know that when I called you. All I knew was that she was here, but now I know that she's in surgery, and she's going to be fine. I'm sorry if I scared you. I didn't have any information when I sent word. I just thought you'd want to be here."

"Of course I'd want to be here. What does appendicitis mean for the baby?"

"The baby? What baby?"

Wyatt rested his forehead on one hand. He was so tired of having this conversation. "Yes, the baby," he muttered.

"Olivia is pregnant?"

"Yes."

"How far along is she?"

"I don't know."

Hudson sat beside him. "Wow, no wonder things have been a bit dramatic for you guys. I had no idea."

"But the doctors will know, right? They won't go cutting into her without a pregnancy test?"

"I'm sure she would tell them anyway, but yes, they do a pregnancy test before surgery." He sighed. "I'm actually really glad this happened, then."

"Why?"

"If her appendix was inflamed, it was only going to get worse, and if it reached a critical point during her third trimester, this would be much scarier."

Oh, then Wyatt was glad too.

"I can't believe I didn't see any signs."

"I don't think she wants anyone to know. She went out of her way to hide the signs."

"But she told you, so that's cool that she trusted you."

"Uh … that's not exactly how it went down."

"She didn't tell you? Then how do you know?"

"That first night I thought she was. It explained why she was marrying a man she didn't love. Or even like. And then she's let some things slip over the last week."

Hudson looked skeptical now, and this annoyed Wyatt.

"Trust me. I don't just randomly make things up. She's pregnant. Anyway, when can I see her?"

He stood. "I'll let you know when she's out of surgery. But I can get you to a closer waiting room if you want. This one can get a little crazy."

It wasn't crazy now, but Wyatt believed him. "Okay, thanks." He followed him to a smaller waiting room with a TV on. He thanked him again and then settled in to stare at an episode of *Blue Bloods*.

The minutes dragged by. His phone told him that an appendicitis surgery usually only takes an hour, and he was certain he'd already been waiting that long, but then he couldn't figure out if he'd started a new episode of *Blue Bloods* or if this was the same one. He'd had trouble focusing on the plot, and there were so many commercials it was enough to drive a man insane.

He prayed the same short prayer over and over, and somewhere during the fifteenth iteration, he realized that he was just as worried about the baby as he was about the mother. How had he gotten so attached to someone he'd never met? He didn't know, but the bond was there.

Just when Wyatt thought he couldn't sit there for another single second, Hudson appeared in the doorway. His expression and relaxed shoulders put Wyatt immediately at ease. "She's in recovery, but you can go in if you want to be there when she wakes up."

Wyatt wasn't sure she'd want him to be there when she woke up, but he didn't think she'd want to be alone, either, so he nodded and stood, his stomach suddenly full of butterflies. There would be no more playing it cool. He now knew that he was in love with Olivia, and this was his one chance to show her his heart.

And though she was a captive audience right now, he wouldn't overstay his welcome. He would say his piece, and then if she wanted him gone, he would go.

Chapter 35

Olivia blinked her eyes open and stared at the ceiling in confusion. That wasn't the right ceiling. Because she was no longer in her motel room. Was she at the ranch? No, that wasn't right either. So where was she?

A dull pain in her abdomen poked a hole through her brain haze, and slowly the details flowed back into her brain: the pain that had woken her up in the middle of the night; her expectation that it would get better—it was just stress, she had assured herself; then the dangerous drive to urgent care; then the ambulance ride to the hospital; lots of questions; the bright lights of the operating room; and then nothing …

Her hand traveled to her abdomen, and gingerly she touched her fingers to a bandage, but not for long as the site was tender.

"Hey," a soft voice said from beside her.

Slowly she turned her head to see Wyatt—her heart swelled so fast she thought it might burst. She couldn't believe what a comforting, welcome sight his face was. Why had she been so mad at him again? She tried to smile but wasn't sure her face obeyed. It felt a little sluggish.

"Nice to see you awake."

"Nice to see you too." Her words came out slow and mushy.

He scooted his chair closer to her bed, and she pulled her arm out from under the blanket in case he wanted to take her hand, which he promptly did.

"You gave me quite a scare, but the doctors say you're going to be fine."

"Good." The strength in her voice surprised her, and she tried smiling again. "Sorry to scare you."

"No, no. You have nothing to be sorry for. So I think you know that I wanted to talk to you, and now you're sort of trapped into listening to me." He laughed uncomfortably.

She squeezed his hand, trying to tell him that she felt anything but trapped.

"So please let me know when the drugs wear off, and then I'm going to take advantage of this situation. But then, if you want me to go, I'll go, I promise—"

"I won't want you to go."

"Really?" His relief was palpable, his smile adorable.

"Really. I'm sorry I got so angry. It was just ... what was *wrong* with you?"

He chuckled. "You're sounding like your old self. Does that mean the drugs are wearing off?"

"I think so. My stomach hurts like the dickens."

"Oh! Do you want me to get someone?" He started to get up, but she shook her head.

"No, I'd rather hear what you have to say." She hoped he was going to give her an acceptable explanation and then declare his undying love for her. She wasn't going to let a little abdominal pain get in the way of that.

"Okay." He took a big breath. "I think we've not done a good job of communicating—"

No kidding.

"—and I think we should try to do better with that from now on."

She waited for the acceptable explanation.

"I should have told you that I was going to go see Brian—"

"What?" she cried with too much volume.

"And you should have told me that you are pregnant."

"What?" she cried with way too much volume. A laugh shot out of her, and it hurt her stomach so much that it turned into a moan.

"Maybe we should wait a minute before continuing this conversation."

"Are you kidding? What are you *talking* about?" Where had this complete nut gotten the idea that she was *pregnant*?

He stared at her, mouth agape.

"Wyatt, I'm about to leap out of this bed and strangle you. Why are you accusing me of being pregnant, and *why* did you go see *Brian*?" She felt herself growing angry and tried to stop it. She needed a clear head. She needed to understand this man's logic.

"Accusing you?" he said slowly. "You *are* pregnant, right?"

"Uh ... no. Definitely not."

He pulled his hand out of hers and put both hands over his face. "Oh no," he said into his fingers. She didn't know if she'd ever heard anyone sound so regretful.

"Wyatt, what did you do?"

Still talking through his fingers, he said, "I told Brian that you were. And Hudson and Seth."

"Wow, you've been discussing my imaginary pregnancy with a lot of folks. What a relief that you didn't talk to Chase about it."

He stared at her, his jaw hanging open an inch. "I am so, so sorry."

"Wyatt, tell me why you thought that I was pregnant." She didn't really care that he'd told Brian his crazy theory. She didn't care anything about Brian anymore. In fact, she found that part of the story kind of amusing. But she did not find the first part of the story amusing—the part where he thought she was pregnant. Sure, she was carrying around a few extra pounds, but she didn't look *pregnant.*

"I'm so sorry." His face resembled a very ripe tomato.

"Tell me why," she said, spacing out her words as if that would make him comply.

He closed his eyes. "That first night, when you were in your wedding dress, I thought ..."

Yep, he was calling her fat. "You thought what?" She was going to make him say it. If for nothing else, so that she could torment him with it for the rest of their lives together.

"Your dress was wet, and it was sort of clinging to you—"

She snorted. She couldn't help it. She clapped a hand over her mouth to hold the laughter in.

He narrowed his eyes. "And you were marrying a man you obviously didn't love, and you were obsessed with getting health insurance, and ... there were so many clues! How are you not pregnant?"

Wow, everything was making so much more sense now. "That's the secret you thought I was keeping."

"Yes! And you said you were crying because you were all hormonal!"

"I never said I was hormonal!" If she had been, she certainly wouldn't have bragged about it.

"Oh. Maybe that's just what I inferred."

"Yeah, it seems like you've been inferring lots of..." *Wait a second. This man liked me. He liked me even when he thought I was carrying another man's child?* "... things. Wyatt, you should have said something." *You silly, silly man.*

"Maybe. But I was trying to respect your wishes. I thought you were going to tell me soon."

She almost snorted again. He would have been waiting a very long time. "And why on earth did you go talk to Brian? Did you think he didn't know?" And did he think it was his job to break the news?

Wyatt groaned. "I was trying to do the right thing. I knew that he was a jerk, that he was a cheater, but he was also the baby's father." He rolled his eyes at himself. "Or that's what I was thinking. I thought that what would be best for the baby would be for the jerk to step up, change his ways, and be a good husband and father."

She studied him. What a complicated man he was turning out to be. There was never going to be a dull moment with this one. "You said that you liked me."

"I did. I do."

"And yet you were going to choose the baby's welfare over your own happiness?"

He nodded. "Thanks for framing it that way. I feel like a total lunatic, and you're making me sound like a hero."

"You are a lunatic." She reached out her hand, and he took it again. "But you're also a hero. I'm sorry everything got so mixed up. I'm sorry I smashed into your barn in a wet, unflattering wedding dress."

A smile tickled his lips. "You looked gorgeous. It was just a little ... clingy." He circled his hand over his own abdomen.

She narrowed her eyes. "Let's stop talking about that part."

"Deal."

She wanted to kiss him. "Wow, what a fun story we're going to have. Too bad we couldn't have just met in church or something, like normal people."

"I don't go to church in Spearfish, and I'm really, really glad that you crashed into my brothers' barn." He got out of his chair but didn't stand up straight. His lips went straight for her forehead, where he planted the sweetest, tenderest kiss. Then he sat back down. "I'm really, really sorry that I acted like a lunatic. I really thought that you were pregnant, and then once I got that theory in my head, I guess I was too stubborn to consider other explanations."

Stubborn was an understatement. "And that's why you told your bothers that you would never, ever be with me? Because you thought I was pregnant."

"You heard that?"

"I heard that."

He looked really unhappy to learn that. "I'm sorry. You weren't supposed to hear that. And yes ... not that a baby would stop me from loving you, but I was thinking that you needed to be with the father."

"Loving me?" Her whole body grew warm. It was a darn good thing her appendix had burst. She'd almost moved to Hot Springs.

"Yeah." He sighed. "Loving you. I know I haven't known you very long, Olivia, but every second I'm with you, I fall deeper in love with you."

"I feel like I've known you forever."

"In a way, I guess we met a long time ago, right? I think maybe God planned for this all along."

"Look at you, you smooth talker."

He chuckled.

"God has a good sense of humor," she said. "I'll give him that."

"I've been saying that for years. Chase disagrees."

She laughed. "We'll work on him."

Chapter 36

When Wyatt offered to let her stay at his house to recuperate, he expected her to argue, but she didn't. She seemed grateful. He retrieved her things from the icky motel she was holed up in and paid her bill. Then he stopped at the grocery store to stock up on healthy foods and things that would help hydrate her. Everyone assured him that she was doing great and would make a full recovery, but he was still nervous.

"So I was thinking," she said when he delivered her bowl of soup to the couch.

"Yeah?" He picked up her feet and slid in underneath them.

"You know, they say a foot rub helps a woman recover from surgery."

He narrowed his eyes. "If you were pregnant, I would definitely offer you a foot rub."

She groaned. "Enough with the pregnancy jokes."

"Sorry. I don't think I'm ever going to stop harassing myself for that."

"Well, you need to. Anyway, I was thinking that now that I'm not mad at you, I was wondering if I could have my job back."

He raised an eyebrow. "Still obsessed with health insurance?"

She pointed at her abdomen. "Do you know how long it's going to take me to pay this off?"

"Not long at all. You might have quit, but I never took you off the payroll. You are completely insured by Honeywood Construction."

Her mouth fell open. "You could have told me that!"

"I didn't want to count my chickens before they hatched. I was waiting to see the paperwork, make sure they were going to pay. And if they don't, then I will fight them, but yeah, you should be covered. Sorry, I didn't know that you were worried about money."

"I'm always worried about money."

He didn't like the sound of that. "You don't have to do that anymore. I'm not a rich man, but I've got enough to take care of you."

"You're such a hero."

He looked at her quickly. "Are you being sarcastic?"

She giggled. "Not even close."

"Well, in that case ..." He pressed his fingertips into the arch of her foot, and she moaned.

"That feels so good." She looked like she might melt into the sofa.

"Finish your soup. You need fluids."

She giggled. "Yes, Doc."

They were quiet for a minute while she ate.

"I don't want you to work for me. I want you to find a job using the gift God gave you." He smiled. "But not at the jail," he hurried to add.

"Okay. But I tried to find a cooking job and failed."

"I know. So there used to be an elementary school in Garrison."

"Yeah?" she said tentatively. "You want me to cook tater tots? That could be just as dangerous as the jail. Those kids can be mean!"

He gently shushed her. "There are no kids. They closed it down last year because there weren't enough kids in Garrison. They decided it would be cheaper to bus them into West Hope."

"Are there *any* kids in Garrison? I've never actually heard of anyone living there."

"A few, yeah, but anyway, the school is owned by the town, and they're renting out their kitchen."

"Yeah?" She still wasn't following.

"I was thinking that you could start a catering business. If my brothers ever get their act together, you could cook for them. But in the meantime, you can do other events."

He could tell that she liked the idea. "I nearly failed high school math, Wyatt. Seriously. It wasn't pretty. I don't know anything about running a business, but I'm pretty sure you have to be able to add and subtract."

"No worries. You have me, and I do know how to run a business."

She was staring at him.

"So what do you think?"

Her hands were trembling, so she put the soup bowl on the end table. "I really would need your help. I don't even know where to begin."

"No problem. Let's start with getting you a new laptop." He chuckled. "Your very first tax write off. Then you can do some research while you finish recuperating. Then we'll get you a website built, and we'll figure out pricing, and get you some booking software ... yeah, it'll be fun."

She pulled her feet off his lap and scooted down the couch to snuggle up beside him. She wrapped her arms around his and nuzzled into him. "You really are a hero, Wyatt Honeywood, and I am so, so in love with you."

He chuckled and caressed her arm. "Even though I'm a lunatic?"

She giggled. "I was wrong, okay? You're not a lunatic."

"Even though I'm stubborn?"

She sighed. "My mother always said that stubbornness was a form of strength, and that sometimes it can be an asset. She wanted me to be more stubborn. I was too much of a pushover, she said, always trying to please everyone else, always trying to make everyone happy." She got choked up and paused for a few seconds. Then, "I wish she could have met you. She would have been ecstatic that I landed such a prize." She looked up at him. "I have landed you, right?"

He laughed. "Yeah, you sure have. And don't worry ..." He rubbed her knee and then let his hand rest there. "I'm sure my stubbornness will rub off on you." He leaned in and kissed her tenderly. "I love you so much, Olivia."

"I love you too, Wyatt."

"Thank you for crashing into my barn."

She giggled. "You're welcome. Anytime."

Epilogue

Olivia trusted Wyatt completely, but she still didn't like being blindfolded. "How much farther?"

He chuckled. "Oh, will you please be a little patient? Just a few more minutes."

"I really think it would have been enough to just blindfold me when we got to wherever we are going."

"I've already told you, that wouldn't work, and you'll see why when we get there."

"Fine." She folded her arms across her chest and resigned to sulk. "Can you at least turn the music up?"

He did as she asked. "You do remember that you asked me to turn it down like five minutes ago?"

"That's because I was trying to listen for clues that would tell me where we were."

He laughed. "Clues?"

"Yeah, like sirens and train whistles."

He laughed harder, which annoyed her. "Train whistles?"

"Yes! Train whistles! It happens all the time on cop shows."

"But you didn't hear any clues?"

"No. I did not." She tried to keep dignity in her voice as she admitted defeat. "I heard a dog bark, but that didn't tell me much."

"You didn't recognize his voice?"

"I did not."

The truck slowed down.

"Are we there?"

"Yes. But keep your blindfold on, or you won't get your present."

In all the excitement, she'd forgotten that he'd promised there would be a gift at the end of this madness. Otherwise, he probably never would have gotten the blindfold on her.

He turned the truck off. "I'll come get you."

She waited impatiently for what seemed like too long, and then her truck door opened. She started to get out, but he said no, that he would take her.

Take her? What did that mean? And then he was scooping her up into his arms, which made her very nervous. She knew he was strong. She'd seen his muscles ripple. But she was no dainty dame.

But she was being carried, and he didn't even seem to be straining. That was good. Grunting would have likely ruined the romance of it all. "Uh, how far are we walking exactly?"

Suddenly, they were in a building. She smelled wood and fresh paint. He gently lowered her to her feet, but she was reluctant to let go of him.

"We are here."

She reached up and yanked her blindfold down, but it took her a few seconds to realize where they were. She gasped. "Oh my goodness!"

"Right? Pretty impressive!"

She scanned the giant room, her mouth hanging open. It looked so different. Still old, but new somehow. And so clean! Her eyes landed on the only wall that actually *was* new. "Wow, you would never be able to guess that a runaway bride smashed her truck through that a few months ago."

"Nope. you sure wouldn't. Did I ever tell you that Chase suggested that night that you might be an apparition?"

She cackled. "What? Are you serious?"

"I don't think he was serious, but you did look pretty creepy standing out there in the pouring rain in your wedding dress."

"Sorry to give you brave gentlemen such a scare. Is that why you came outside? To see if I was real?"

"No, I came outside because you were smokin' hot, and I didn't want one of them to get to you first."

She laughed and leaned into him, playfully elbowing him in the side. "We need to find some womenfolk for your brothers too. I guess I need to start making some girlfriends in West Hope."

Wyatt clicked his tongue. "I don't know. Hudson might already be on to something. The other day he said he saw the most beautiful nurse he's ever seen. Old Doug Cotton's granddaughter, I guess. He sounded quite smitten."

"Well, good." Her eyes traveled across the beams overhead. "This looks so great, Wyatt. Nice job. Does this mean that Chase has given in?" She thought this would be good for Chase, but she still felt bad if he was being railroaded into something. The longer she knew Chase, the more she liked him, and the more protective she felt of him.

"He hasn't exactly *given in,* but they've decided to move ahead with the project anyway."

She couldn't believe it. She had all but given up on her wedding venue idea.

"They've already got the first wedding booked, believe it or not. It's nearly a year from now, but Hudson has already asked me if you'll cater it."

"What, he was scared to ask me himself?" She knew this wasn't true. She was just messing around.

"No, I think I was just around, so he asked me. Is that a no?"

"Of course I will!" She was so excited she was bouncing. "Wyatt, this is just the best thing ever."

He took her hand and gently spun her toward him. He looked nervous all of a sudden. When he went down on one knee on the brand-new floor, she knew why. Her hands flew to her mouth. She'd suspected this was coming, but she hadn't expected it yet.

From out of nowhere, he produced a small velvet box. "I don't think you know this, but today is exactly six months from when you drove into this barn."

She giggled. No, she didn't know that. It felt like a lot more than six months. That whole ordeal felt like it had happened in another lifetime, maybe even someone else's lifetime.

"So I know we haven't known each other very long, but I want to make it official. We can have a nice, long engagement if you want—"

She couldn't wait. She fell to her knees and threw her arms around his neck. He hadn't even opened the ring box yet, and it ended up wedged between the two of them as she pressed her lips to his. She pulled back to say, "Yes!" and then kissed him again.

He pulled away laughing. "Yes to the proposal I haven't said yet or yes to the long engagement?"

She laughed too as she pulled away from him. "Sorry, please finish your proposal."

He cleared his throat and opened the box. "Olivia, would you do me the honor of cooking me suppers for the rest of my life?"

She barked out another laugh. "Yes, but ask me right!"

He grinned. "Olivia, I love you more than I ever thought it would be possible to love anyone. Please be my wife. Let's have a family and have fun and laugh a lot and maybe even fight a little and then grow old together."

"Wow, you've really got this whole thing planned out." She reached down and took his hands, pulled him to his feet, and then kissed him again. "Yes, of course I will do all of that, and I will definitely cook you supper." He looked so pleased with himself that she added, "At least three nights a week."

He laughed and leaned his forehead against hers. "Deal."

Willow White Books

Bannon Ranch Romance
The Cowboy Billionaire's Enemy
The Cowboy Billionaire's Secret Baby
The Cowboy Billionaire's Ranch Hand
The Cowboy Billionaire's Snowstorm
The Cowboy Billionaire's Best Friend
The Cowgirl Billionaire's Bodyguard

Honeywood Ranch
Marry Me, Cowboy
Know Me, Cowboy
Protect Me, Cowboy
Remember Me, Cowboy
Forgive Me, Cowboy
Love Me, Cowboy

www.ingramcontent.com/pod-product-compliance
Lightning Source LLC
Chambersburg PA
CBHW032217070925
32253CB00016B/163